W9-DIJ-010

Sioux Slaughter

Sioux Slaughter

Chet Cunningham

Thorndike Press • Chivers Press
Thorndike, Maine, USA   Bath, England

NEW HANOVER COUNTY
PUBLIC LIBRARY
201 CHESTNUT STREET
WILMINGTON, N C 28401

This Large Print edition is published by Thorndike Press, USA and by Chivers Press, England.

Published in 1998 in the U.S. by arrangement with Chet Cunningham.

Published in 1999 in the U.K. by arrangement with the author.

U.S. Hardcover 0-7862-1643-3 (Western Series Edition)
U.K. Hardcover 0-7540-3579-4 (Chivers Large Print)
U.K. Softcover 0-7540-3580-8 (Camden Large Print)

Copyright © 1998 by Chet Cunningham/Book Crafters

All rights reserved.

Thorndike Large Print ® Western Series.

The text of this Large Print edition is unabridged.
Other aspects of the book may vary from the original edition.

Set in 16 pt. Plantin.

Printed in the United States on permanent paper.

British Library Cataloguing in Publication Data available

Library of Congress Cataloging in Publication Data

Cunningham, Chet.
    Sioux slaughter / Chet Cunningham.
        p. cm.
    ISBN 0-7862-1643-3 (lg. print : hc : alk. paper)
    1. Dakota Indians — Wars — Fiction. 2. Large type books.
I. Title.
[PS3553.U468S56 1998]
813´.54—dc21
                                                        98-30795

Sioux Slaughter

1

Hays, Kansas: Spring, 1868:

Buffalo Horn's already bloody knife paused just a moment at the white man's forehead as the Brulé Sioux looked into the terrorized blue eyes. Then the sharply honed steel cut into flesh arcing halfway around the scalp on one side and in a bloody, flashing movement slicing around the other side.

A bellowing scream tore from Sam Freening's throat as the knife completed the circle. Then Buffalo Horn's left hand jerked forward and down expertly and the scalp popped from the rancher's skull. The Brulé Sioux roared his war cry, leaped high in the air and tied the brown hair under his surcingle.

He crouched, as alert as an antelope, eyes scanning the ranch yard, seeking any danger or a new target. The barn burned fiercely a hundred feet from him. The frame house was not on fire, yet.

Two warriors rushed out of the house with cloth and dresses. One warrior wore a tattered gray army jacket and a blue military hat. Another nearly naked Brulé wore a woman's sunbonnet and a frilly polka dot blouse.

Buffalo Horn saw a second white man scalped near the well. The white woman lay nearby, naked, spreadeagled and tied to stakes driven into the ground. A warrior came away from her adjusting his breech-clout, yelping in satisfaction. A second warrior knelt between the pure white legs and thrust at her crotch savagely.

The older Brulé with the fresh scalp knew what was more important right now for him. He ran to a shed near the house and pulled open the doors. At once he saw what he wanted — two double bitted axes and a four-foot steel saw to cut logs. Beside them lay a most prized possession, four flat files that would cut into and sharpen the stolen white eye's metal that Buffalo Horn would use to make arrowheads and lance points.

He grabbed them all, ran to his horse and lay them in a small pile, then put one of his personally marked arrows on the tools and the prized files claiming them for his own.

Buffalo Horn looked around again. The ranch had been an easy raid. The two white men had been taken down at once and the woman had been no match for the warriors.

8

There were five children. He saw a warrior run out of the house with a baby in his hands. The Brulé held the year old child by the feet, whirled around in a circle and screeched in delight as he threw the baby as far as he could. The infant hit the edge of the shed where her neck broke and skull smashed. The warrior gave a cry of victory.

Buffalo Horn raced inside the house. He had seen someone go in with a burning torch. If he were to find any woman things for his wives he must look quickly. The strange white man's lodge with several rooms had been torn apart. He found a metal cooking pot and three sharp knives which he grabbed and hurried to the next room. For a moment he stood still, listening.

Sound came from a bed. He bent and stared under it until he could see in the darkness. There was movement.

With his stolen pistol ready, Buffalo Horn advanced on the unknown warrior and was ready to shoot.

He lifted a blanket and saw a small girl with long blonde hair and blue eyes stare out at him. She was about four summers. He grabbed her by one hand and pulled her out. She said something to him he didn't understand, but she didn't seem afraid.

9

When he knelt beside her, she balled her tiny fist and hit him in the nose.

Buffalo Horn laughed in surprise. This white eye was strong, brave for a woman. He would keep her.

The Brulé carried the small sunflower-haired girl under one arm and ran out of the house as the next room burst into flames.

He sat on the ground near his pile of loot and looked at the child. Chief Running Bear had always wanted a white eye child. He would like this woman child with hair like sunshine. Quickly he lashed her wrists together, then tied her ankles. He put her over his back like a blanket roll and tied her wrists and ankles together across his belly. She would be safe and secure there.

Buffalo Horn gave a high, sharp cry. The warriors looked up.

He motioned toward the corral which had been spared. Six of them ran to the pen and opened a gate. They urged the thirty horses out calmly and away from the fire. Then six more Brulé warriors rode up and herded the horses away from the ranch, moving them slowly northward.

Another six Brulés on horseback gathered up ten of the white man's buffalo with the long, dangerous looking horns, and drove them to the north behind the horses. Buffalo Horn had hesitated about taking the cattle. The animals the white men called cows were not as valuable as the buffalo, but they would furnish a change of food, he had decided.

Buffalo Horn gathered up his loot, tied it together with thongs and carried it as he rode north. The small girl slung over his back cried, but he ignored her. They had a hard ride to get back into safe territory. There was no time to worry about small slaves.

Soon Buffalo Horn realized the cows could not be driven as fast as horses could. If they kept the plodding animals it would take them twice as long to reach their camp. He shrugged. For now they would keep the ten cows, and decide later whether to let them go.

Behind the escaping savages, Sam Freening lay flat on his back in the farmyard dirt on a warm Kansas morning and tried to sit up. He couldn't. His legs wouldn't move. His whole head was on fire. Blood spilled down his face from the sliced flesh on his forehead, narrowly missing his eyes. He lay with the back of his head on the ground, one arm thrown over his chest. Sam hurt so terribly that he had to fight down total panic.

His next thoughts were for his family. He

11

had seen the heathens grab his wife. Sam closed his eyes and swore not to think about it. Her torture and rape had been too brutal and painful for him to think about right now. But what about the rest of them? He had seen George shot down and scalped. Where were the children?

Wave after wave of unbearable pain slashed through his head and his chest where he had suffered an arrow wound. *He had to fight it down!*

What had happened to his children?

Sam knew he was badly hurt. He couldn't think about the knife he had seen at his temple. He thought the savage would slit his throat. Why hadn't he? The cascading, continuous, sickening pain boiled through his body again.

Now it never left. He couldn't bear to wonder how much he had been sliced up by the knife. If he didn't move they would think he was dead! Yes, play dead. Now, what could he see?

Sam focused on the well, then the burning house.

He wanted to scream, but he couldn't. Why?

Was he really dead?

No, he couldn't be dead and hurt this much. A wave of burning, white hot flames seared through his head and he wanted to vomit, but he couldn't. He had never felt this kind of pain before. It was the continual burning of a branding iron on raw flesh!

Sam shuddered, then brayed a terrible scream of rage, but not a whisper of a sound came out of his mouth. He tried to roll over, to sit up, to shout — nothing happened. Slowly he realized nothing on his body worked! He couldn't move, couldn't shout. The only parts of him still functioning were his eyes and brain.

Through the pain and the dust of the ranch yard, Sam saw his Megan, his four year old wonder child. A savage held her under one arm, then he bound her across his back. At least she wasn't dead.

Christ no! Not his Megan! His little girl wasn't dead, she was worse than dead. Megan had been captured by the savages! Sam tried to scream again. Nothing came out of his mouth. He couldn't even cry!

None of the Indians running around his ranch noticed him.

He must be dead.

Then his only partly functioning brain touched a memory cord and he saw the glinting knife again, the grinning savage as he pressed the blade against Sam Freening's forehead.

God no! He had been scalped! Oh God! Some men lived through scalping. He'd seen a man once who had. He was pitiful, a freak without a mind, a vegetable people had to feed.

Most people were dead before they were scalped. Why hadn't he been? Why was God making him suffer this way?

Sam lay there unmoving, his breath coming slowly, as his diaphragm forced his body to breathe. Blood continued to run down from his forehead. He had seen pictures of scalped bodies. They all had a large circle cut off the top of the head. Scalp and hair all gone, just a bare white skull showing with traces of tissue and angry red clots and smears of blood.

Sam tried again and again to blink, but he couldn't. More blood seeped down his forehead and this time it ran into his right eye, blinding it. He couldn't blink it away. He couldn't lift his hand to wipe it clear.

He looked out at all that was left of his world from his left eye. It was slightly higher off the ground. The barn burned brightly in the early morning sun. His wife! Where was Agnes? What had happened to her?

Oh, God! He remembered! The filthy, raping savages!

Where was Ginny, his fifteen year old girl,

and the other children?

A warrior ran into his view swinging something. When he threw it Sam saw what it was: Becky! His baby! She flew through the air and hit the shed near the house. He could almost hear her skull as it crushed. He saw her tiny body fall into the dirt. He knew Becky was dead.

For the first time he realized that he could hear nothing. No sounds of any kind came through to his brain. He must be dying.

Oh God! Why? Why his family? How had he sinned so terribly against God that He had brought this kind of retribution and punishment down on him and his family? Why was God taking such an awful toll against them? Fury mounted in Sam. If he could only rise up and kill the bastards!

Another warrior, naked except for a cloth over his crotch, ran out of the house dragging Ginny. Already the savage had torn off her dress and the chemise covering her breasts. Ginny was bare to the waist and her face distorted with what must be a scream of anger and terror.

Sam still could hear nothing.

The warrior pushed Ginny to the ground and tore at her tightly fitting drawers. After a moment, the Brulé took out his knife and cut the crotch out of the drawers, then fell on top of the fifteen year old and probed. Sam saw his little girl's body shaking and stiffen in pain as the savage entered her.

Tears streamed down her face. She beat him with her small fists but the Indian didn't seem to feel it.

Someone rode by on an Indian pony and motioned to the brave on the ground. He gave a final thrust, raised his knife in victory, and then slashed Ginny's throat with his bloody knife. He pulled out of her, quickly lifted her long blond scalp and ran out of Sam's range of vision. Ginny's crumpled, bloody body spasmed once, then lay still.

God, please let me die! Sam Freening pleaded silently.

Three Indian ponies galloped toward him. One went around, one jumped over him, the third pony came down with one large hoof directly over his chest. Sam saw the hoof coming but couldn't move. It drove down lower and lower until it touched his chest and then slammed through his ribs, driving the splintered bones into his heart, finally killing Sam Freening.

Zeke Udell stared at the smoke coming over a low hill and kicked his limping horse into a faster walk. That was too much smoke for a chimney, somebody must be in trouble over that way. Trouble for others sometimes led to a windfall for Zeke Udell.

Zeke pondered that thought for a moment. Not that he was a man who took advantage of others. No sir! But, say a body was to find a ten-dollar gold piece in the dust beside the trail. Now that little round of gold wouldn't do a living soul any good just resting there. The man who lost it surely wasn't coming back to find it, so it just made plain ordinary horse sense to pick up the ten dollars and use it. Stands to reason.

Zeke looked over the rise at the small ranch below. He was less than a quarter of a mile away and at once he knew what had happened. Even from there he could see a body lying in the farm yard. The barn had burned down to a few embers. The house was still burning, but nothing inside it now could be saved.

He kneed the mount into a trot and reined in at the well where he ground tied his horse and stepped down. The two women were naked, scalped and dead. Both had been used, he imagined. A broken arrow beside one scalped man told him all he needed to know. They were probably Sioux renegades.

Zeke squatted down and checked the man to be sure he was dead. He'd never seen a man live through a scalping, but some did. This one was long gone to his reward. Zeke went to his knees beside the man, scowled a moment, then shrugged and dug into the dead man's pants' pockets.

He found a long snaptop purse in the man's back pocket. Zeke looked around, saw no one, then opened the leather money holder. His eyes widened. The gent had two twenty-dollar bills all folded neatly in one side of the purse. In the other side of the snaptop lay three twenty-dollar gold pieces and some small silver change.

Jumping catfish . . . a hundred dollars! He took all of it, but one twenty. That would indicate there wasn't a robbery. Zeke stuffed the purse back in the pants' pocket and looked for weapons. The blamed Indians had run off the stock, so they must have taken all the weapons they found as well.

Zeke paused by the young girl who lay on the ground face up, slit throat, scalped. He stared at the young breasts with pink nipples and areolas. Probably had been a virgin who never had a chance at life. He saw the cut out crotch of her cotton drawers and snorted. Some savage had been in one damned big hurry.

At the house he found it was still too hot to try to poke through the remains. Hell, he had more cash money than he had seen in five or six years. He'd just head on into Hays and report what he'd found, get a good room and a bath and then he'd see if there was a young lady of ill repute who might want to haul his ashes all night for two dollars!

Zeke mounted up and pushed out a little faster. He could buy a fresh horse in Hays. The little town was close by. He'd ridden this grub line twice before. Zeke was glad that the grub line was fast becoming an institution in the West. Nowadays, almost any of the ranches would give a man a meal and a place to sleep, even if the owner didn't need a new hand. Zeke had been taking free handouts this way for almost a year now. Sure as hell beat working.

It was slightly before noon when Zeke pulled up at the small wooden building with a second story false front and a sign over the door that said: Hays Town Marshal.

Inside he found one man with his feet propped up on a battered desk, his hat over his eyes, and his hands folded on his generous belly.

"Mornin' stranger, what can I do for

you?" The voice was muffled by the lawman's hat.

Zeke tried to see the man's face but couldn't. No use. He shrugged. "Just want to report a massacre. Little ranch about six miles northeast of town. Don't rightly know the name of the spread. Didn't see no brands showing."

The hat fell on the floor as Marshal Lloyd Menville kicked his feet off the desk and came upright.

"Bodies? Buildings burned?"

"Right. I saw four bodies, could be more. Girl, maybe sixteen, man about forty, scalped. Another man younger who also lost his hair, and a woman, maybe about forty."

"The Freening place. Only ranch out that direction I know about is Sam Freening's Bar-F. Not a big spread, just one hired man. Was the stock missing?"

"Right. Corral empty. I'm no tracker, but it was plain the horses and some critters were driven off in a bunch. They didn't just scatter."

"Damn, I know the Freenings. Right nice people." Lloyd shook his head. "Me, I can't do a thing about it. Out of my jurisdiction. You best ride out a mile to the fort, Fort Hays. They got the Indian problem to deal with."

20

Zeke turned his low crowned black hat in his hands. The Stetson was still dust covered from the trail.

"I been riding four days. Kind of thinking about a bed and a bath and some good cooked food. . . ."

"Up to you. Army will want to know about it. Usual they send a scouting party out to look around. Might even hire you as a scout for the day."

Zeke scrubbed one hand over his face that had a month's growth of scraggly beard.

"Hell, I guess it's my dooty. Much obliged."

Fifteen minutes later Zeke stood in another office, this one the Commanding Officer's of Fort Hays. The fort was a gathering of frame buildings needed for army operation in the area. They had been built around a central square which functioned as the parade grounds. There were no palisades, none were deemed necessary in this Kansas area where there was little trouble with frequent Indian attacks.

Zeke had been taken to the commander's office at once. The plate on the door read: Colonel Paul Adamson, Fort Hays Commander. Zeke told his story to three officers in the room. The army men talked together for a moment, then two left at once. Zeke could hear shouted orders outside the office.

"Mr. Udell, to be sure we find the site of the attack without delay, I'm authorized to pay you two dollars to lead us back to the ranch. Will you be available to take on this task?"

Zeke looked at the colonel and shook his head. "Colonel, I'd rather not. Been considering some good food, a bath and a soft bed in Hays."

"It won't take a lot of your time. It's barely past midday. We'll be out there in two hours at the most. Then you'll be paid and free to continue on your way. I'm told you have a lame horse. We'll furnish you with an army remount for the trip out and back. We move smartly on these short trips."

Colonel Adamson had eagles on his shoulders indicating his full colonel's rank, and wore his army uniform proudly. He was 42 years old and had been in the army his entire adult life. But now he was stuck here in an out of the way post and his chance of hooking his career to a general who could pull him along with him was remote.

Paul Adamson was short and stocky, standing just five-four and weighing a solid 180 pounds. He was clean shaven except for mutton chops and a full moustache. Now he preened the lip hair and stared at the civilian.

"Well, Mr. Udell, have you made up your mind?"

"Sir, yes. I'd feel a lot better about it if I could get you to the ranch as quick as possible. I'll go."

As he said it another officer came in. He was much taller than Colonel Adamson at two inches over six feet. His lean, hard form held 185 pounds of well developed muscle. His brown hair was full for an army man, and he sported a full moustache. He held out his hand.

"Colonel Colt Harding, Mr. Udell. Any idea what tribe might have hit the ranch?"

"No, sir. Not really. I'm not much on Injuns. Saw a broken arrow that looked like it could be Sioux."

Harding nodded and looked at the colonel. "Sir, I'll be riding along with the detail, if it's all right with you."

A flicker of resentment crossed the senior officer's face, then he relaxed. "Glad to have you along. I've authorized an investigation only. No pursuit. They'll have had twelve, fourteen hours head start before we could get into the field. If there's to be a chase, it will come later, after we know more about it."

"Yes, sir," Colt said and both he and Zeke Udell headed for the door.

The detail of fifteen men, two sergeants, a Second Lieutenant and Lieutenant Colonel Colt Harding rode into the Sam Freening ranch just after two o'clock. Colt had pushed them into a trot and eaten up the six miles to the ranch in under an hour.

Two civilians were already on the site. Colt rode up to the older of the two.

"Sir, you know who these people are? Can you positively identify them?"

"That I can, Colonel. I'm Oran Stafford. I hustled right out here soon as I heard. Known Sam and his family ever since they got to town. This is . . . *was* . . . the Sam Freening family. We found four of them and the hired hand, George. Haven't found the four-year-old, Megan, yet."

"How many?"

"Five bodies so far, should be six."

Colt nodded at Stafford. He was a medium sized man wearing lace up boots, blue jeans and red suspenders. His face was about the color of the braces. He seemed genuinely shaken by the deaths.

The troopers helped, but after two hours

of digging through the ashes of the ranch house and the barn, they could not find the body of young Megan Freening.

Colt had assigned ten men to dig the five graves. In back of where the house had been, there already stood a plain wooden cross. It read: "Baby Freening. 3 days old. Died January 6, 1867."

Stafford read a simple ceremony over the graves, then the troopers filled them in.

Colt took a scouting ride around the ranch. He found the tracks of the horses and cows heading almost due north. He made a note on a pad of paper he carried and rounded up the troops, heading them back to the fort.

Oran watched them go. He and the other man from town decided there was nothing else to do. They rode back into town silently. Oran still couldn't put the sight of the naked, ravished Freening girl out his mind. She had been a beauty. Next year, when she turned sixteen, he had planned on courting her.

Back in town, Oran headed for the Outlaw Saloon. He slid up to the bar and ordered a whiskey.

Vince Lowe owned the small saloon that had a bar along one side, a dozen poker tables, but no fancy women. It was a drinking

man's saloon. Vince was 29 years old, unmarried, tall and slim as a ten-cent cigar. He
loved to wear gussied up suits and did
whenever he was not behind the bar. He
fancied himself a gambler, but usually lost
most of the money he made selling drinks in
his own poker games.

Now Vince grinned at his friend. "Little
early for you to be hitting the whiskey, isn't
it, Oran?"

"You didn't see the Freening family!
Butchered, scalped! Christ, I never want to
see anything like that again. Damn Injuns
should be wiped out, shot down like wild
animals!"

Vince pushed a mug of beer down the bar
top to Oran.

"Easy, easy. Let it settle down a little.
Probably the damn Brulés. They get nasty
in the Spring and Summer."

Oran downed the whole mug of beer
without taking a breath, then gulped in a
lungful of air. He belched at once.

"Somebody should *do something about
them butchering heathens!*"

"Sure, and we all should have a couple of
easy women on the side. What should happen, don't always."

"We could take care of *one* blithering
murdering Indian. He's right here in town."

Vince snorted. "That Brulé kid, the half-wit who mucks out over at Charlie's?"

"Why not? He's Indian. Damn Indians just killed six people I knew, the Freenings."

"You better have another beer, Oran."

Oran wasn't listening to his friend. "We know where the little savage sleeps, out behind Charlie's saloon, right?"

Vince nodded, his brows lifted. "Hey, you are serious about doing in the kid, ain't you?"

"Fucking right! Soon as Charlie closes. I'll be drunk enough by then. Send me another beer with a whiskey chaser!"

It was nearly midnight when Charlie closed his saloon that night. A half hour later the Indian boy Charlie called Daylight stepped out the rear door of the saloon and listened to Charlie close and lock it. He headed for the small shed at the side of the saloon building where he slept.

Daylight had been in town six months. He had wandered in one day wearing the traditional breechclout and nothing else. He was out of his head with a fever and Charlie nursed him back to health. The fever had burned out part of Daylight's brain. He couldn't speak, not even Sioux talk. He moved slowly, followed Charlie around like a puppy, and seemed content to be the swamper at the saloon. Charlie fed him, and gave him some cast off clothes, and had himself cheap help.

Vince Lowe and Oran Stafford had been drinking and planning all afternoon and evening. By midnight both had been drunk and sobered up and started getting drunk again.

They both strapped on gunbelts and took knives and a rope. Then they slid down the alley watching for Daylight. When he came out they both laughed so loud he heard them, but he turned away into his hovel.

Vince knew he became mean when he was drunk. Everyone told him about it, so he tried to stay just short of getting that mean drunk. But tonight he was far into the mean side and he was pleased.

Oran became more stolid and angry when he drank. Now he walked with deliberate steps toward the shed where Daylight had vanished.

"Son-of-a-bitching little bastard of an Injun!" Oran said over and over again as he walked. "You a son-of-a-bitch of a little murdering bastard, and we coming to get you!"

Vince looked at him in the half moonlight and giggled. He never knew how he could giggle and be mean at the same time. He pulled open the door to the shed and saw a candle burning inside.

Oran dove through the door, grabbed the startled Daylight by the front of his shirt and dragged him outside. Daylight was not more than fifteen and weighed less than a hundred pounds. Oran drove his fist into the boy's face, smashing his nose, splattering blood over his clothes and face.

Daylight never talked. No one knew if he didn't choose to, or if he didn't know any English, or if he had some kind of speech problem. Now he gurgled in anger and his arms flew up to protect himself.

Vince came up behind Daylight with his knife out. He sliced the kid's shirt down the back, nicking the red skin in a place or two. Then when Daylight turned, Vince ran a blood line with the sharp six-inch knife across the young Brulé's cheek.

Daylight jumped away from him right into Oran's arms. He gripped the frightened Indian boy in a bear hug while Vince ran two more shallow slices down Daylight's half bared back.

Daylight bellowed a scream of rage and jerked away. He crouched by the wall, looking for a way out. Never before had two white men attacked him. He moved one way, but his mind couldn't command his body to function quickly. Daylight had taken only two steps when Vince tripped him. Vince kicked him in the side, then in the stomach, and Daylight curled into a ball in the dirt waiting for them to kill him.

"You damn Injuns like knives, right?" Oran hissed, as his knife cut a deep gash on Daylight's arm. "Remember how you raped that pretty little Freening girl?" Oran cut him again on the other arm.

Daylight struggled to his feet but hesitated, not sure in his foggy mind which way to run. Vince kicked him in the crotch and saw the Indian go down again, groaning from the pain of two smashed testicles.

Oran snorted when Daylight couldn't stand. He picked him up, slung him over his shoulder and carried him toward the livery barn half a block down.

The entire town of Hays, Kansas, was only two blocks long. It had some twenty businesses, and perhaps thirty houses. The merchants had built for the future. The livery stable was the only two story building in town.

Vince and Oran had agreed how they would do it. They carried Daylight to the hayloft over the stables and brought down the rope from the pulley at the top of the mow door. The rope was usually attached to a giant fork which was buried into a load of hay and lifted a large bite up and into the mow where it was swung in place and the fork loosened.

Now Vince cut the rope off the heavy fork and tied what he thought was a proper hangman's noose. Carefully, he fitted the noose over the partly conscious Daylight's head, cinching it up tight around his neck.

They spent two minutes judging the fall to the ground, adjusting the rope through the pulley at the top of the mow door, and then tied off the half-inch rope solidly.

"Guess it's time," Oran said, suddenly more sober than he had been for hours. "Goddamn Indians don't get to do all the killing around here."

"Yeah," Vince said. "This one is for all those Freenings. I knew them. Damn sweet little girl they had."

The men looked at each other.

Vince giggled. He pulled out his knife and slashed Daylight's face twice. Blood gushed.

"Now," Oran said. Together they lifted the Brulé Indian boy and dropped him out of the hayloft mow door.

Daylight dropped straight down for six feet, then hit the end of the rope. The pulley ground for a moment, but held.

31

They both listened but did not hear the Indian's neck snap. His body hung there a moment, still six feet off the ground. Then Daylight turned toward them. His face slanted upward at them, but his neck had not broken.

That's when they remembered they had forgotten to tie his hands behind him. Both his hands gripped the rope over his head, but he couldn't lift himself. He tried to pull himself up to relieve the pressure of the rope around his throat. A moaning scream came from his throat. His breath came in ragged gasps. Then the air whistled through his mouth. Soon it turned into a series of gagging coughs and then a long gurgle. Finally, one of his hands dropped away, and soon the other.

He swung there a moment, his body slowly turning six feet off the ground. Then they heard a rush of air from his lungs. A death rattle. Daylight had at last strangled to death.

Vince and Oran climbed down the ladder to the ground floor of the livery and went outside. They both stood looking up at the body turning slowly on the rope, and then walked away in different directions toward their houses.

Both men were now stone cold sober.

2

Town Marshal Menville swore roundly for two minutes as he stared up at the body hanging from the Hays Livery haymow door. It was not quite six A.M. and he wasn't used to being out this early before he'd had his breakfast.

Lloyd Menville was two inches under six feet, 42 years old, and the part time town marshal because nobody else would do the job. He had a thick shock of prematurely white hair, a square jaw, and a glare in his eye that kept everyone from calling him Whitey. To further enhance his rough appearance, Menville shaved once a week, letting the stubble grow from Sunday through Saturday night. It was Tuesday, so he was still fairly presentable.

The stable boy at the livery had banged on Marshal Menville's house door a half hour before rousing the part time lawman from his warm bed.

Now at the livery, Menville swore softly.

"Christ, get up there, Willy, and cut him down. Untie the damn rope, something. Don't want half the town to see poor old Daylight hanging there."

The stable boy nodded and ran in the big door and up the ladder to the mow. He found where the rope had been tied off and loosened it until the body came to rest on the dirt outside the livery.

Marshal Menville pulled the poorly tied hangman's knot off the corpse and frowned at the slashes on the body. Willy came back with a horse blanket and spread it over Daylight.

"You say he was hanging there when you come to work, Willy?"

"Yes sir. Just like you saw him. I went home about ten last night cause Mr. Johnson said I could. I closed up and left the one night lantern on, just like Mr. Johnson. . . ."

"Yeah, yeah, Willy. And you didn't hear nor see nobody at that time?"

"Right. Daylight warn't hanging there then."

"You see how he was slashed and cut up? This was more than just a killing, Willy. It was a damned execution. Probably for what happened to the Freenings yesterday. I been afraid of something like this ever since Charlie took in the kid."

34

They stared at the blanket a minute.

"Willy, you go hitch up a rig and bring it around. Want to haul Daylight over to the undertaker before we get a lot of folks staring at him. Hustle, now, boy."

By ten that morning everyone in Hays knew about the lynching. Millicent Gail Kane arrived at the Marshal's office at ten-fifteen.

Millicent closed the door softly, turned around and fastened the gaze of her green eyes on Marshal Menville. She was a tall woman of 24 years, trained as a school teacher, a Civil War widow and now living with her brother until she could get the fall term of school opened in Hays.

"Yes, Mrs. Kane. May I help you?"

"It's outrageous, Marshal! To think that anyone in this town would . . . would torture that poor, simpleton Indian, and then . . . then lynch him! This is not the deep south. We are not overrun with problems. I hope you have caught those terrible men who did this to Daylight."

"Ma'am, understand how you feel, but this is a matter for the army. I don't have jurisdiction over Indians. Not a thing in our law books about any of the Indians. They are a U.S. government problem, that means the army out here in Kansas. I suggest you go talk to Colonel Adamson out at Fort Hays. He's the man to see."

"That murderer! Last year he attacked an Indian Village and killed twelve people, three of them women and children!"

"I really doubt, Mrs. Kane, that the army considered it murder. The Indians who haven't moved to the reservation are considered an enemy force, a foreign element. None of them are citizens. I can deal only with citizens or legal aliens, like if they come from Mexico or England or somewhere."

"That's ridiculous!" Millicent snapped.

"Yes, ma'am. But I'm afraid that's the way it is."

Marshal Menville appreciated a pretty woman and Millicent Kane certainly filled the requirements. She had long brown hair that framed a pretty face with wide set eyes, a snub of a nose and a soft creamy complexion that saw little of the hot Kansas sunshine.

"You will do nothing, then?" she asked, her black high button shoe tapping on the floor.

"Nothing I can do except cooperate with the military authorities."

"Good day, Marshal Menville. This is ridiculous. I will go to see the colonel. Then I'm going to write to my United States Senator and demand some action!" She turned so quickly that the long dress she wore spun, revealing brown matching stockings over the tops of her black shoes.

Her hand darted down to lower her skirt, her chin lifted and she marched out the front door.

Millicent Kane glared at Colonel Adamson where she stood in his office at Fort Hays.

"What do you mean, you don't have any jurisdiction? He's a Brulé, an Indian. The Indians are the *only reason there's a fort in this area*. How can you say he does not come under your control?"

"Mrs. Kane, the subject is dead. If he were alive and causing problems, *then* he would be my responsibility. Since he's not bothering anyone, I'm not authorized to take any action."

"Not against him! I want you to find out who murdered that poor boy. He's a human being, just like you and me. Maybe he had been ill and had no education —"

Colt Harding stepped into the commander's office.

"You called me, Colonel?" he said when the woman standing there broke off her angry words.

37

Colonel Adamson grinned. "Matter of fact, I did. Colonel Harding, I'd like to present Mrs. Millicent Kane. She's our new school teacher at Hays as soon as the school year starts this fall."

Colt held out his hand, quickly saw that she would not shake it, and nodded instead.

"Ma'am. It's a pleasure."

She barely bobbed her head at him, then moved a step closer to the commanding officer's desk.

"Colonel Adamson! Somebody in town tortured and then cold bloodedly *executed* that young handicapped boy by hanging. You mean to tell me you aren't even going to investigate?"

Colonel Adamson stood and walked to his small window that looked out on the parade grounds. Then he came back. "Mrs. Kane, I'm a busy man. We have nearly six hundred men here to utilize the best way we can in the best interests of the United States and the entire population of the state of Kansas and surrounding country. I'm just a simple soldier who follows orders. What I'm going to do for you is to let Colonel Harding explain the fine lines between what the army can and can't do regarding Indians and the civilian population.

"Colonel Harding has the ear of General

Sheridan, and I'm sure can set your mind at rest concerning this matter. I have to check on the quartermaster, so why don't you use my office?" He stood and before Mrs. Kane could reply, left the room and closed the door behind him.

Millicent turned to Colt, her green eyes twice as angry now that she had been shunted to an underling.

"Colonel, do you know about the Indian boy who was tortured and murdered in Hays last night?"

"Yes, Mrs. Kane. Do you know about the six white people who were tortured, raped, beaten, shot, scalped, slashed and otherwise disfigured before they were killed by a band of at least thirty Brulé or Sioux Indians yesterday at the Freening Ranch? Or the one year old baby who was thrown against a wall by the Brulé savages until her skull smashed open like a melon and her neck broke."

"That's hearsay. That's. . . ."

"That's the truth, Mrs. Kane. I was there yesterday. I saw it. I saw the burned down barn and house, where twenty to thirty horses had been before they were stolen. I helped bury five people and now we are afraid that the four-year-old girl from the family has been stolen as a slave by the Brulé. Does any of this touch your tender sensibilities about inhumanity to man? As you say, those were human beings — those Brulé Sioux Indians — who slaughtered that family, stole their horses and burned down every building in sight."

Millicent staggered and sat quickly in a chair. "I . . . I hadn't heard, not for sure. I know how these stories build. . . ."

"Ask Sam Freening how it feels to be scalped. This story did not build."

"I'm sorry. I'll pray for them."

"That's not going to help Sam a hell of a lot, is it?"

She stood, the glint in her eyes just as strong. "Nor will it help the Brulé boy called Daylight. But I will pray for his soul as well. Perhaps I should start now by praying for your soul, Colonel. I should have known it was useless coming here again."

"You've protested something like this before?"

"Of course. Someone has to stand up for the American Indian. We are stealing their land, murdering their warriors, and treating their women and children as if they are nests of rattlesnakes."

"Mrs. Kane, have you ever lived in an Indian village?"

"Well, no. Of course not."

"Why not? Try out their life style, see

40

what you're missing. Watch the women work from morning until night and grow old and withered and sick and dead at thirty-five. Watch the babies die because it's a hard winter and they are short on food. Watch the women nurse their babies for four or five years and grow older each day. Watch the women do all of the work in moving camp while the men sit their war ponies and watch. I think you'd enjoy the rites of passage as an Indian woman."

"I think I'll be riding home now. Will you bring up my horse?"

"How can you defend these people so fiercely when you don't have the slightest bit of information about them; when you know nothing of their lives, their habits, or their way of life?"

"How? The same way you ride into their villages and kill anyone you see. Because I *want to defend them,* just as you want to kill them. Have I asked you your rationale for your wholesale slaughter of an entire race of people?"

She marched out of the room, found her horse and rode away from the fort without a backward glance.

Colt watched her go, shook his head sadly as he realized there was a lot of truth in what she said, but there was not much he could do about it, one way or the other.

Colonel Adamson came back in snorting. "Finally got rid of the damned Indian-lover I see. What the hell is her problem?"

Colt shook his head.

"Well at least you're good for something around here." The Fort Commander lit a cigar. "You know, I've never been happy about Sheridan sending you out here to spy on me, or whatever the hell you're doing."

He waved as Colt started to say something.

"Yeah, yeah, I know. You're a specialist on Indian fighting. Well, I guess we should use you then. Got to thinking about that damn raid yesterday. You said you never did find a body or even what might be a body of that four-year-old. Chances are damn good that she was stolen by the Brulé. Goddamned Sioux like to take young kids and turn them into Indians. With her long blonde hair, some damn chief would go wild to have her as his kid."

Colt tensed when the kidnapping was talked about so plainly.

Colonel Adamson looked up. "Oh, sorry, I forgot about your own daughter. She was taken by whom, the Comanche? Right. Damned crude of me, I apologize. But I think we better put together a detail and go out and see what we can find.

"Want you to lead it. Take thirty men. Troop C hasn't been tested lately. Take the whole damn troop and see what you can do."

"Yes sir. I'd like to take five Indian scouts."

"Five? What the hell for?"

"Hunting. We'll see if we can live off the land. That way in future patrols we can cut down on needed supplies hauled along and we can move that much faster."

"That damn Lightning stuff, huh?"

Colt grinned. "Deed it is, Colonel. I hear you've got a fledgling Lightning troop here. Haven't talked to them yet, but I'll get to it as soon as I get back from this one."

"We've got some Pawnees we use now and again. I'll have five of the best brought in."

"Good. Who is the Troop Commander of C?"

"Gent named Lieutenant Abner Eliason. A good man."

"Fine. We'll leave at dawn tomorrow."

By seven-thirty the next morning, the line of troopers, four abreast, moved out from the Freening ranch heading north. Colt had out two scouts, one a mile ahead of the

43

troop, another three hundred yards.

The other Pawnee braves were put on hunting detail. Colt explained to them patiently before they left that he wanted to live entirely off the land. Birds, rabbits, fox, any stray deer they might find, but no beef, no buffalo.

Colt settled into the four-mile per hour stride of the army mounts and yearned for the faster pace of the Lightning troop. At last he made a compromise with himself. Fifteen minutes out of each hour they cantered. It added almost a mile an hour to their four-mile rate of travel.

The trail was easy to follow. Colt pushed the men with only short breaks. Instead of stopping at four in the afternoon the way most cavalry troops did, he kept them riding until almost dark, gaining another fifteen miles on the savages.

Colt talked with his lead scout, Short Grass, who knew a little English and Lieutenant Eliason. The gist of it was that the Brulés were moving slow because they had from six to a dozen head of beef along. They couldn't gallop the beef and it took some work to herd them along since the Indians were not used to the behavior of the sometimes balky and cantankerous range beasts.

"We might catch them before they get to

their summer camps," Colt said. "Most beef won't move more than ten to twelve miles a day. We've got a chance."

"How far did we come today, Eliason?"

"Almost fifty miles, I'd say. More distance than these men have ever done before in a day."

"Wait until tomorrow, Lieutenant."

The Pawnee hunters came back to the column an hour before it stopped. They had fourteen rabbits, six grouse and ten pheasants. There would be half a rabbit or bird for each man. It was three times what they usually had to eat on the trail. The men who had been griping at the long ride grinned when they heard about the fresh meat.

Colt checked the sentries about midnight. It wasn't his job, but he wanted to be sure the men were alert. Three of them challenged him, but the fourth one was sleeping. He called Lieutenant Eliason who kicked the private back to the main camp and replaced him.

The next morning the Boots and Saddles call came promptly at 5:45 as usual and by six they were on the trail. Quickly the track shifted sharply to the west. There was no apparent reason. The entire herd still moved together, and it was obvious that the Brulés were not making good time. The troop had passed three camp sites yester-day. With any luck Colt and his troopers could catch the hostiles today.

They had crossed the south fork of the Solomon River the day before and now before noon they came near the north fork. They had found another camp, as well as the picked clean carcass of a steer. The Indians were eating as they went and left the rest of the steer for the wolves and vultures.

Just after a quick food stop, the lead scout came back with interesting news.

The Pawnee, Short Grass, talked half in sign language and partly in Sioux with a few English words. "Trail split two-hands-full ways," he told Colt.

Colt ticked off each finger and his thumbs. "Ten ways, trail split?"

Short Grass nodded. "Each trail shows cow and horses."

The game had changed. The hostiles knew they were being followed. They must have one warrior watching their back trail. Now they were splitting up so most of them would get away. It would work. It almost always worked.

Colt got the troops back in the saddle and pushed them hard to the split up point two miles ahead. Colt let Short Grass pick out the best target and they rode again following the meager trail of what the scout said was one steer and eight or nine horses that seemed to be tied together.

Short Grass took a fresh horse that one of the hunters had been riding, and galloped back to the point. Colt had brought his twin .45 Colt revolvers with the pearl handles. They rode on his hips ready for action. He had a Spencer repeating rifle in his boot and six tubes of ammunition loaded and ready to replace the seven round tube now in the Spencer. It loaded through the stock and was quickly replaced to give the company more fire power than the single shot breech loaders.

An hour later Short Grass let them catch up to him.

"Just over hill. Three Brulés, ten horses and the cow."

Colt, Lieutenant Eliason and Short Grass rode ahead to recon the situation.

"They'll leave the cow and charge forward the moment they spot us," Colt said. "Eliason, you take ten men and ride hard down that swale behind the brush and get ahead of them. When you're in position light a fire and throw up some smoke. That will be our signal to charge them."

Eliason grinned. "Yes sir. Three of them should be no problem."

"You've fought the Sioux before, Lieutenant?"

"No sir, but the odds. . . ."

"Don't mean a damn thing if you're the one man in the company killed. Remember that, Eliason. Now get your men and ride."

Colt kept the rest of the company in sight of the target. He worked through light brush and around the rim of a valley to stay concealed.

Just an hour after they had left, Lieutenant Eliason and his men put up a smoke a half mile ahead of the Indians.

Colt brought his men up and drove forward, still in a column of fours. When they broke free of the brush a quarter of a mile from the three Indians, they spread out into a troop front in a wide arc two hundred yards long and swept forward.

The Brulés ran. They tried to drive the horses with them, but at last broke and charged straight ahead to take advantage of as much distance as they had.

Lieutenant Eliason had spread his men twenty yards apart across the small valley. He heard the shots as Colt and his men charged. Now Eliason sat his horse behind a large cottonwood tree and watched the three Brulés riding straight into the trap.

He had ordered his men not to fire until

the savages were thirty yards from the line. It was unnerving to wait, but Lieutenant Eliason held, and when he estimated the distance at thirty yards, he bellowed: "Fire!"

One of the Brulés fell on the first volley. The second charged straight at Lieutenant Eliason. He saw the savage lift his bow. The Brulé did not even have a rifle! Lieutenant Eliason wanted to laugh, but he sighted in and fired. He missed!

By then the charging red man was no more than twenty yards away. The arrow string twanged and Lieutenant Eliason heard it as he tried to sight in again on the Indian. The arrow slammed into his thigh and brought a gush of pain and a scream from the officer.

Eliason fired his weapon, but the Spencer had not been aimed, and the Brulé flashed past him at only fifteen feet. Clearly, Lieutenant Eliason saw the fury on the red man's face. He was nocking another arrow but there was no chance to fire backwards at his enemy.

By the time Lieutenant Eliason got his mount turned around, he heard two shots and the Indian who had wounded him tumbled off his horse and lay still.

Sergeant Denver rode up and caught

Lieutenant Eliason's mount by the halter.

"You're hit, sir!" Sergeant Denver said. "We got two of the three, the other one got through us somehow."

Lieutenant Eliason hadn't said a word, he could only stare down at his thigh where a Brulé Sioux arrow had lanced into his flesh.

"I'll help you down, sir, and we'll see about that arrow."

Lieutenant Eliason hardly heard him. The wound was painful, but not deadly. He shuddered. Never before had he been wounded. Not even in the tail end of the big war with the South. He let Sergeant Denver help him down from his horse.

"You'll be fine right there, sir. I'll help the men round up these horses and tell the Colonel about your wound."

Lieutenant Eliason stared at the arrow. What was the procedure, break off the arrow? Yes. Could he do it? Probably. He grasped the arrow and a new wave of pain cascaded through his system. For a moment he thought he would faint, but he fought it off.

When he looked up again, Colonel Harding reined in beside him. The leader of the patrol swung down and looked at the wound.

Without a word, Colt put both hands on

the arrow and broke it off three inches from his leg. Lieutenant Eliason looked up in surprise.

"I never even felt that. How did you do it?"

"Takes practice. The first two or three times it's best to practice on yourself." He nodded. "You're damn lucky, Eliason. That Brulé was aiming at your chest. Your mount must have surged upward at just the right time to bring up your leg to take the arrow. You'll live. You stop all three of the hostiles?"

"No sir. Sergeant Denver said one of them slipped through. They split up when they came at us."

Colt scowled as his head bobbed. "So now whoever they are out there know that we came this far after them. We could cut another trail and try again, but I don't think we will. Not with this troop. If I had my Lightning Troop I'd be all over them within twenty-four hours."

Sergeant Denver came up and saluted.

"Sir, we have captured eight horses, and now have them in a contained area. The steer is grazing. Sir, two of the horses have army brands on them."

"Thanks, Sergeant. Tell the men we'll eat here. You ever slaughtered a steer?"

"No sir," Denver said grinning.

"Find a farm boy who knows what he's doing and get that steer butchered. Save the liver for me. Everyone gets to cook steaks over an open fire until he's stuffed."

They would stay there the rest of the day, Colt decided. That would give them time to get Lieutenant Eliason back on his feet and realizing that he could ride again. The men would get all they wanted to eat, plus steaks to carry with them until noon the next day. That was about as long as the beef would hold in this warm weather.

Going home would be slower driving the horses. No, they would put them on lead lines behind eight troopers. No problem.

Whispering Feet had swung low on the far side of his war pony as he came toward the line of soldiers firing at him. This way only one of the troopers would have a shot at him. He felt hot lead zapping over his head, heard the cry of pain from his war pony, and then he was through the screen of brush and riding hard up the small stream behind a line of young cottonwoods and willow.

He had seen his two companions shot down. Their medicine had not been as strong as his. Whispering Feet would stop and thank the gods as soon as he could, but right now he had to ride. He felt of his war pony and looked at him, but nowhere could he find any wound.

Twice he checked behind him.

He could see no one following or chasing him. Still, they could follow later. He slowed his mount, moving into the stream and walked upstream for as far as he could before the waterway became choked with brush.

Then he rode hard again to the west and north. He crossed Prairie Dog Creek and turned upstream. He rode past the small falls and the lightning struck cottonwood. After a five minute ride, he came to the summer camp of Running Bear's band of Brulés. He was back among his people. He would have to tell of the deaths of his two friends. Soon there would be much wailing and keening and slashing of breasts and arms in mourning.

Whispering Feet went straight to Chief Running Bear's tipi. Several of the other raiders had already returned including Buffalo Horn.

The squat, thick chested Buffalo Horn looked at Whispering Feet and scowled.

"Small Fox and Beaver Tail?"

"Both shot down by the Pony Soldiers. Both killed by Captain Two Guns! He has returned to haunt us!"

There was an immediate outburst of chatter by the warriors. They had heard many tales from their Ogalala Sioux cousins about the mighty Captain Two Guns, the Pony Soldier who rode and fought with two pearl handled pistols, one on each hip. He could ride a hundred miles a day like an Indian. He did not use the bugles or wagons. He fought like an Indian. Captain Two Guns was said to have such great medicine that no arrow or lance could penetrate his body!

He was renowned as a great warrior who had been plaguing the Indians of the plains for a year now. Why had he chosen to come to Kansas to attack and kill the Brulé? He had been in the land of Chief Red Cloud during the winter. Why was he here now?

Whispering Feet told of his escape, and the loss of ten horses and the white man's buffalo, then he went to the widows of the two dead warriors. He must somehow give each of the four women gifts.

Chief Running Bear heard the reports of all of the warriors and then talked with Buffalo Horn well into the night. After the other warrior left, the chief went to look at his new daughter.

The small one would be called Sunflower, in honor of her golden hair. She would not be a slave, she would be raised as his daughter, with his other children. Chief Running Bear stood tall for a Brulé, almost five-feet ten. He had learned much English from a slave woman he had owned for several years. At last he had sold her to a trader for three rifles.

Now he pushed back the buffalo robe and watched the small white eye girl with the hair like the sun. She turned over in her sleep and mumbled something. She would want for nothing. She would grow up with her long hair properly braided and out of the way, and she would some day marry a great new chief and take a proper place in the life of the Brulé Sioux tribe. She was a good sign from the gods!

She was a sign that the Brulés would grow and prosper, that Pony Soldiers would be defeated, and that the white eyes would be pushed out of the traditional buffalo ranges and their prime hunting areas.

He looked around and saw no one watching him. Cautiously, Chief Running Bear bent and brushed his lips across the golden girl's cheeks. She mumbled something, and Chief Running Bear lifted up smiling.

It was a good day to be alive!

It was a good day to be a Brulé Sioux! It was a good day!

3

Colt Harding changed his mind sitting there on a grassy bank of the small stream a hundred miles from Fort Hays.

It was barely after three in the afternoon. The steer had been butchered, the choice cuts taken out and cooked. It was a quick process when the thin slices of beef were held over a fire on a forked stick.

At three-thirty he ordered the men to pack up. What was left of the beef was cut into quarters, and two were wrapped and packed on one of the captured horses.

"We move out in five minutes, Sergeant Denver," Colt told the non com. "We'll ride until dark, but don't tell the troops how long we'll be in the saddle."

Lieutenant Eliason sat up where he had been resting. Colt had tended to his wound the best he could. The bleeding had been stopped but it was a bad place for an arrow. The head was out of sight in tender flesh.

"We moving out because of my wound?"

Lieutenant Eliason asked.

Colt watched him for a moment, then nodded. "Yes. In two days that's going to be nasty, festering, infected. I don't want any gangrene. That would mean you'd lose the leg."

Lieutenant Eliason looked up sharply. There were no one-legged officers in the army. He scowled and touched the bandages near the wound. "Can't you get the arrowhead out?"

"You've seen an arrow in that deep before, Lieutenant. It takes some cutting, a lot of care, and a physician. I don't qualify. We'll ride with you in the lead. When you need to stop, we stop."

They rode until seven-thirty and a deep dusk. They could not canter because of the lieutenant's wound, and as a consequence covered only about seventeen miles.

That night, Colt lit three candles and examined the wound again. When he took the bandage off it began to bleed.

"Take it out, Colonel!" Lieutenant Eliason blurted.

"It will hurt more than anything you've ever felt before," Colt said, worry tinging his voice and making it harsh.

"I know. I'd rather hurt now than lose the leg."

"I could cut something I shouldn't and you'd still lose the leg back at the fort." Colt stared at the young officer's face, saw the determination there, and at last agreed.

First he honed his pocket knife, the three-inch thin blade, until it was sharp enough to shave. Then he called the two sergeants and a corporal.

Sergeant Denver listened to the needs, and came back five minutes later with a pair of dry sticks and a bunch of hollow reeds that he bound together to make torches. The two biggest men in the company came and sat down waiting.

Colt cut a hole in his spare blue shirt and spread it over Lieutenant Eliason's leg with the broken arrow coming through the hole. He enlarged the hole in the shirt around the wound and nodded to Sergeant Denver.

The two big privates came up and knelt beside their troop commander.

"Lieutenant, this is going to hurt," Colt said. "Scream if you want to. These men will hold you as still as possible. I'm sorry we don't have a quart of whiskey for you."

Colt pointed at the big privates and one held each shoulder, the two sergeants held his legs down. Two more men lit the torches and when they blazed up enough so Colt could see clearly, he grasped the arrow shaft.

A shrieking scream from Lieutenant Eliason was more than the enlisted men had expected. His body writhed with the pain. Colt jiggled the arrow shaft again and suddenly the screaming stopped.

"He's passed out, what I hoped for," Colt said. "No man can stand that kind of pain for long." He used the pen knife then, probing around the wound. He found the wings of the arrow an inch under the flesh. Colt cut carefully, slicing flesh and wiggling the arrow. He had one side almost out and saw the other projecting wing of metal hooked on a thin blue tube.

A vein or an artery!

Carefully he cut around the tube, pushed the arrowhead deeper into the flesh, twisted the shaft and pulled upward again. This time the rear wings of the arrowhead missed the blood tube and a moment later the rusted bit of metal slipped out of Lieutenant Eliason's flesh. Blood flowed from the wound and Colt at once pressed a folded white handkerchief over the bleeding spot and pressed down firmly.

Colt gave a sigh.

"Now hold him, I still need to bandage it." He had folded up two of his best white handkerchiefs and now placed the second one directly over the one he had applied before. With strips from his cut up shirt, Colt wrapped the white compress in place. Then he wound more and more strips of the blue shirt cloth around his leg until no more blood showed through.

The third torch lit the fourth and Colt watched the leader of C Troop. Colonel Harding dug into his saddlebags and came up with a thin silver flask. Colt knew Lieutenant Eliason would need the whiskey more now than before the cutting.

Colt soaked a cloth in a canteen of water and washed the lieutenant's forehead, then gently slapped his face. The officer came around slowly.

"My God that hurts!" Lieutenant Eliason burst out, sweat beading his face. He blinked and looked around. "Hey, what the hell happened?"

"You passed out just the way you were supposed to," Colt told him. "Until the army gets that new fangled ether stuff to put you to sleep, we have to use pain and shock."

"It's out? The arrowhead is out?"

"Right, and you have a hefty hole in your leg. At least you won't lose it. Now, we'll put some blankets on you and you get some sleep. That and some more steaks for breakfast and you may make it yet."

He did.

Lieutenant Eliason insisted on riding all the way back to Fort Hays and they arrived just before mess call at the end of the second full day.

Colt took the wounded man at once to the post physician, Captain John Constatine. Colt gave him a quick run down on the wound and treatment while the sturdy doctor in his forties unwrapped the makeshift bandages.

"Sounds like you did everything I could have under the circumstances," Dr. Constatine said. He scowled. "And you're right. I've ordered the new ether compound on every requisition I send in but the brass back in Washington doesn't seem to think anesthesia is a necessity out here."

He unwound the bandages and took off the white pad and growled. "We have a little bit of infection, but I think we can take care of that. If that metal arrowhead had been in there right now I'd be fighting to save your whole damn leg. I'll use some of my magic potions and have you back on duty in no time."

"Colonel Harding," Lieutenant Eliason said, "thanks. I owe you a lot."

"I'll send you a bill," Colt said gruffly. "As soon as that leg heals I want you to put a thousand rounds into some targets. From what you told us, one well aimed round would have taken down that hostile before he got his arrow off. Don't worry about the cost of the rounds. General Sheridan thinks every man in uniform should have target practice and better weapons training. For now, you settle in for some good duty here in the infirmary."

Back in the doctor's office a few minutes later, Doc Constatine held out his hand.

"That boy should have lost that leg, you being two days and more away. Where you learn to dig out arrowheads?"

"A lot like digging out lead slugs."

"You with the North?"

"Nearly five years dodging bullets and Reb Rangers. But I lived through it."

"I did two years with the Massachusetts Fifteenth Regiment as a surgeon." He shook his head and looked out the window. "After the excitement, the . . . the life and death struggle of battle . . . the shock, the horror . . . really living on the dangerous edge months at a time . . . civilian life was a terrible bore for me."

He waved Colt into a chair.

"I had a civilian practice in Boston for a

year, treating little old ladies with boils on their backsides and crazy imaginary female complaints that they could never tie down. Made more money than I had ever seen before. But I was so nervous and jittery and irritated by the waste of a doctor, the need lessness of it all, that I came back in the army. They knocked me down to Captain, but I didn't care. You come over for dinner tonight at six. My wife always has one or two extra in. We can talk. Were you at Shiloh, The Wilderness?"

Colt shook hands with the medic and hurried to the Fort Commander's office to give a quick verbal report while his orderly heated up his bath water. He didn't want to be late for the Doctor's dinner.

Dinner that night with Dr. and Mrs. Constatine was a pure pleasure, the food was delicious and Colt ate far too much. It was good talk about the big war, the REAL WAR. The doctor's wife was short and round, loved to cook and loved to eat, and was content to live anywhere the army sent her husband.

Colt finally got away about nine, went to his quarters and dropped into bed.

The same night the patrol got back, Major Bainbridge had bowed to his seventeen-year old daughter Juliana's insistence to have a small dinner party so she could invite two young officers she was interested in. Juliana had been on the post only three months, arriving with her mother after a stay in Chicago.

The guests included the two young and unmarried lieutenants, and two married officers and their wives who were new to the post. It would be a small welcoming party. The dinner came off without any problems. Juliana even helped her mother serve, then sat down between the two young men who were sending angry glances at each other.

Lieutenant Ben Danalaw, commander of A troop, sat on Juliana's right. Ben had gone through West Point, graduated a year before the war was over and flew into battle after battle as if he were trying to get himself killed. He wasn't even wounded.

Now three years later, he tended to think through a problem before charging in to solve it. Juliana was such a problem. Ben stood five ten and was trim in his uniform. He had black hair, a thin moustache and snapping black eyes.

He caught Juliana's hand and stared deep into her soft blue eyes. "Miss Juliana, the invitation is still open for that picnic I told you about. Lieutenant Pearlman and his wife

64

will be along and we're planning on driving down to the Smoky Hill River and do some splashing around."

"Now, Ben, don't press me. I said I'd think about it. Land sakes, it's just days and days until Sunday. I said I'd think on it and I will."

She took her hand from his and turned the other way where Lieutenant R. J. Turnball sat rather stiffly. He wore glasses, had errant locks of brown hair that refused to lay down in any pattern, a rather long nose and a firm jaw. He also was about five-feet ten and a trim figure in his uniform. His assignment was as a Second Lieutenant in infantry, a platoon leader in George Company. He was twenty four years old and had been an officer only for a year now. He had no battle experience at all.

R.J. had a full beard that he kept trimmed close to make him appear older, and a furious desire to make good in the army.

When Juliana turned to him he was surprised. R.J. had expected to see little of her, what with Ben on the other side. Ben was a good conversationalist. Everyone said so.

"R.J. you've hardly said a word and here we're almost ready for our dessert. Have you enjoyed the dinner?"

"Yes, Miss Bainbridge. It's really quite

excellent. The stuffed pheasant was most delightful."

Juliana tittered. The way R.J. spoke always amused her. But he was so darkly good looking.

R.J. swore silently at himself for sounding like a boob! How could he do that? When he was near a girl as pretty and interesting and as *nice* as Juliana, his mind turned to mush. Sometimes he couldn't even talk.

For a moment he thought he was mistaken, then he felt it again. Juliana had touched his leg with hers! Under the table he felt her leg again. It rubbed his leg and she looked at him smiling sweetly. "What are your plans for this Sunday, R.J.?"

Mush! He couldn't think of a thing. Her leg rubbed his again and he thought he would explode. He looked away and said the first thing that came into his mind. "I'm not sure, but I think I'm duty officer that day. I'm not sure."

"Oh, I see." Her leg came away from his. "Well, that's too bad. If you do have the duty, then I guess your social calendar is just already filled up. R.J., maybe the Sunday after that. You did promise to teach me how to play bridge. Everyone is learning to play and you said you knew."

"Yes, sometime soon."

R.J. wanted to beat himself about the head and shoulders with his own fists. How could he be such a ninny?

Juliana smiled at him and turned back to Ben. She wouldn't dare rub her leg against his. She smiled at him and leaned slightly toward him so her dress would show even more of the cleavage between her breasts.

"Ben, I think I'll be able to go on that picnic after all. Did you say just after ten o'clock sometime?"

"Indeed I did, Miss Juliana. I'll get a picnic basket from the officers' mess for the four of us."

"That's so thoughtful, Ben. Now, I better help mother serve dessert."

She started to get up and both lieutenants pushed back to help her. They bumped together getting her chair back and glowered at each other.

Major Bainbridge saw the confusion and came to the rescue. "So, Lieutenant Danalaw, I understand you've taken on the task of putting together our very own Lightning troop?"

Danalaw sat quickly holding himself ramrod straight as he had at West Point. He was sure the Major would understand.

"Yes sir, I most certainly am trying. So far I just don't have enough information."

"Didn't you know the man who started the first Lightning troop is right here on post? Lieutenant Colonel Harding is your man. I'd expect he'll be talking with you when he gets situated."

"Sir, I'm a little confused about exactly what Colonel Harding's position is here at the fort," Lieutenant Turnball said, determined not to be shut out of the conversation with the adjutant and number-two man in command of the whole fort.

Major Bainbridge chuckled. "Fact is, both Colonel Adamson and I have been trying to get an answer to that same question. There certainly is no table of organization position for him here. Actually he's on TDY, Temporary Duty, and assigned here by General Phil Sheridan himself."

"I've heard that General Sheridan is a bit unpredictable," Lieutenant Ben Danalaw said. "What do you suppose he's planning?"

"Who knows? My guess is that Phil will soon be our Commanding General of the whole Military Division of the Missouri, from Chicago to the Great Salt Lake, and from Ft. Brown at the bottom of Texas all the way to the top of Montana and the Dakota territories."

"Some say that the lack of treaties with the Indians may mean a fall and winter campaign against the renegades," Lieutenant Turnball suggested. "It does seem possible."

"That would put Colonel Harding in a good listening post for General Sheridan. My own dispatches don't reach Phil directly. That could be one reason for Harding to be here."

The women brought in the dessert, a German chocolate cake. Generous portions were cut and placed on delicate bone china plates.

"Now, no more army talk," Mrs. Bainbridge said. "We should be talking on a more cultural level. Do either of you young gentlemen play bridge?"

"R.J. knows how, Mother," Juliana said, touching his arm. "He's promised to teach me to play Sunday after next. Isn't that exciting? Then we can have bridge games just almost every night!"

Mrs. Bainbridge smiled at the young man. He was almost blushing. "Lieutenant Turnball, I heartily approve. I tried to teach her the fundamentals, but evidently her mind was on something else. Be stern with her and insist she learn about No Trump."

When dessert was finished they all retired to the small parlor and sat in the modestly stuffed furniture. It wasn't grand, it was army issue, but comfortable enough.

Lieutenant Danalaw seated Juliana and whispered to her, "What's all this fawning over R.J. when you said you'd come on a picnic with me?"

"Ben, really," she whispered back. "Just because we're having a picnic doesn't mean I can't be nice to other men. Besides, there are a lot of fish in the sea, and ducks on the pond."

"Juliana, you are a tease."

"Am not," she said quickly, then smiled at him and as he sat down she turned to Lieutenant Turnball on the other side of her.

"R.J., just what does No Trump mean?"

Ben Danalaw seated himself in the chair and glared at Juliana, then began talking with Mrs. Bainbridge, telling her again how delicious the meal was. But all the time he was watching Juliana with R.J. She was laughing and giggling and touching his arm and leading him on.

How could she do that after accepting his invitation for a picnic? He would never understand her. Yet she was so pretty, so fresh and bouncy like a puppy, so damned desirable — so, so unused. He wished they had a piano or a fiddler so they could dance. Ben just wanted an excuse to hold the lovely girl in his arms.

"So, Lieutenant Danalaw, we'll have to arrange a bridge game," Mrs. Bainbridge said. "You do play, don't you? How about Tuesday next week? We'll have two tables, I think. Do you suppose that you could possibly come?"

"By all means, Mrs. Bainbridge. I'm no expert at the game but I want to learn to play better. I would hope that you could arrange for Juliana to be my partner."

"We'll see about that. We usually draw for partners, but with inexperienced ones, we almost never team them. It isn't fair and the play isn't as good. We'll see."

At eight-thirty, Major Bainbridge cleared his throat and stood. The young officers took the hint, said goodbye to the ladies, shook hands with the Major and walked outside. Not twenty feet from the Major's doorway, Ben stopped. "Turnball, that was a damn impolite stunt you pulled in there just now."

R.J. turned, frowning. "I don't see where you have any complaints. You're the one with the engagement for a picnic with Juliana."

"That's what I mean. I have an arrangement, and you barge in and take up all of her

71

time talking about bridge."

"Just because you wouldn't know a Grand Slam from a No Trump, don't get nasty, Danalaw. Anyone can see that she was talking to me just to make you angry. If I had any sense I'd know that I should bow out right now. I don't have a chance with the young lady. I've seen how she looks at you."

"Sure, sure. She talked with you for the last hour. Is that supposed to tell me that I have the inside track with her? That's crazy. I want you to just back off, Turnball, leave my lady alone!"

Lieutenant Turnball laughed softly. "Now that does it. I was ready to quit the race, but now, by damn, I won't. You don't have the right to order me around, especially where Juliana is concerned. Now I'm going to try harder than ever to win her."

Lieutenant Danalaw snorted. "Watch your trail, I might have to ride right over you. It wouldn't be much loss. I intend to have that girl, Turnball, so watch yourself at all times!" He did a smart about face and marched to his quarters where he went in and slammed the door.

The next morning, Colt slid into a chair in the Fort Commander's office. Major

Bainbridge and Colonel Adamson were already there. A large scale map of the northwestern corner of Kansas was displayed on the map wall.

"New orders, gentlemen. Now that the Kansas Pacific Railroad is completed all the way through Hays, we get our army dispatches from our headquarters at Ft. Leavenworth regularly and much more often. General Phil Sheridan wants a complete inventory of the savages in this area, their strength, what the mood is, the number of raids and attacks on whites, and generally what the tone and activity is of the hostiles not on the reservations. We'll be sending out some additional patrols. Comments, gentlemen?"

"Hope headquarters realizes that we just can't run out there and make a census count of the hostiles," Major Bainbridge said. "So how the hell are we supposed to come up with all them facts?"

"Have to do the best we can," Colonel Adamson said. "We can count summer camps, count tipis and figure one warrior a tipi. That be about right, Harding? You've been in the field more lately than both of us."

"Yes sir, about right. As you know, the women put up and take down the tipis, but they have to have a man to hunt for them and protect them. Most widows move in with a sister or take another husband. So the tipi comes down or goes to someone who needs it."

"Let's hope we can create thousands of new Indian widows," Adamson snarled. He picked up the dispatch. "Listen to this. It's from General Sherman, our Army commander."

" 'Indian troublemakers not on the reservations deserve to be soundly whipped, and the ringleaders in any trouble hung, their ponies killed and such destruction of their property as will make them very poor.' "

Colonel Adamson preened his moustache and glanced up at the other two men. "This is starting to sound like the soft talk is over, that the brass is getting ready to launch an all out winter attack as soon as the snow ties up the hostiles in their winter camps."

Colt stretched out his legs and laced his fingers together behind his head. "I'd guess that Sheridan is going to concentrate any action down into Indian Territory south of Kansas, and over into the Texas Panhandle. He knows there is going to be a whole passel of Cheyennes and Arapahoes down around the Canadian and the Washita Rivers.

"Up here we won't have so much trouble

from the hostiles, and we'll also have a freer hand. We should be able to play it about any way we want to."

Major Bainbridge shifted in his chair. He looked at Colonel Adamson who nodded vigorously at him.

"Colonel Harding, would it seem impertinent if I asked you about your orders? I've never before seen a set of military orders cut quite the way yours were."

"Oh, how do you mean, Bainbridge?"

"The wording. Temporary Duty I understand, but the rest of it puzzles me. 'He will be posted to Fort Hays, and there to render such assistance, aid and leadership as may be required by a military post in a region with known and numerous group of renegade Indians and hostiles.' That is the part I just can't figure out."

Colt chuckled. "Sounds like Phil Sheridan. He told me he wanted me out here to check out the area, not to countermand any orders or actions Colonel Adamson is taking. I'm sort of the spare wheel on a wagon, there if I'm needed. I expect when the winter offensive against the hostiles starts, I'll be long gone from this part of the country."

Colonel Adamson nodded, his face showing that he was reasoning it out. Soon he nodded. "All right, I can accept that.

Normally I outrank you, but anybody traveling on orders signed by a Major General carries a lot of weight."

Colt held up one hand. "Yes sir, I know what you mean, but I'm just here for the ride, and to kick some life into any Lightning troops I find that are forming. I hear Lieutenant Danalaw has started one here for you."

"True," Major Bainbridge said. "He really doesn't know what to do. Anything you can do to help him will be a boon. He called for volunteers but the men didn't know what they were volunteering for. You know how a man hates to leave a troop where he's been for even two or three years."

"Fair enough, I'll get on it first thing in the morning, if the Colonel doesn't want me to take a run on one of the survey patrols he'll be making."

"I'd rather have a sharp Lightning troop, Colonel."

"Yes sir. In two weeks, you'll have one."

That same morning, Oran Stafford, who owned the Stafford General Store, and his buddy Vince Lowe, proprietor of the Outlaw Saloon, sat in the back room of the store sipping cold beer that Lowe had brought over.

"Damn, I never seen no hanged man twitch and jerk the way that fucking Indian did," Oran said stroking his full red beard. "You see that? He wiggled and squirmed for two, three minutes before he finally died."

"It warn't no clean hanging, for damn sure, but who cares?" Vince sipped at his beer. He wore his usual saloon gambler's outfit of black suit, fancy vest and string tie. "Quit keeping me in suspense, Oran. You get the goods in or didn't you?"

Oran took another pull at his brew, smacked his lips and wiped his mouth on his sleeve. "Take a gander over here. You're almost a rich man!"

Oran opened the top of a foot square by four feet long wooden box. Inside lay a dozen breech loading rifles. There were three different makes of weapons, and none of them was new.

"We got two boxes like this. Some Remingtons, and a few Phoenix Cartridge rifles and then some Peabody .433 center fire weapons. All single shot breech loaders, but the damn customers ain't gonna know the difference."

Vince picked up one of the weapons, a Peabody, and checked it. "Damn sure they ain't new." He tried the breach mechanism and then pulled the trigger. "At least they work. That contact of mine is still fresh and just waiting our word."

"Then partner, I guess you better get moving. He's Cheyenne?"

"Hell, no! He's a Southern Brulé Sioux, just like that crazy kid we hanged. He's a sub-chief of some kind. He got lost one winter, damn near froze to death before he was took in by some rancher and learned to speak English before he went back to his tribe. Now he's a big stick in some band north of here."

"Yeah, but how do you tell him we're ready to talk business?"

"Smoke signals."

"The hell, you say! You send smoke signals?" Oran laughed.

"Not all that hard. All I got to do is go up to the south fork of the Solomon River and make a fire. I put on some green brush to make lots of smoke and then smother the fire with a wet blanket. I get it burning again and send up another smoke. I sent up three smokes within ten minutes or so. That's it."

"Mean somebody is gonna be watching all the time?"

"He told me somebody would see it and the word would get around."

"What the hell's this savage's name?"

"He's got a good one, Sly Fox."

Oran finished the beer and belched. "Damn, that's good!" He looked up at his friend. "Well, let's do it right now. I'll ride with you. Might see some pheasants on the way up there so I'll bring my scattergun."

"Sounds reasonable." Vince paused. "How much we gonna get for each rifle? We never did set a price."

"We trade the rifles for horses. I'd say ten horses for each weapon."

Vince shook his head. "Doubt it. Sly Fox said he'd never paid more than four horses for a rifle."

"But he's the one buying. He needs them. Let's set it at five horses, take it or leave it."

"He'll go for that," Vince said. "This redman really wants those rifles. We can sell the horses to ranchers for at least thirty dollars a head. That's a hundred and fifty bucks per rifle. How much they cost us?"

"Six to seven dollars each!"

"Damn! We gonna make a hundred and forty dollars a rifle! What's that times twenty-four?"

Oran took out a stub of a yellow pencil and did some arithmetic on a brown paper sack. "That's three thousand, three hundred and sixty dollars pure profit!"

"I'll be gee-hawed! That's more cash money than I ever heard about. I don't

79

make that much profit in five years running the saloon. We'll be rich men."

"Near enough." Oran grinned. "Now see why we had to hang that Injun? If anybody gets wind we had a hand, it'll only build our reputation as real Indian-haters who wouldn't do nothing to help the bastard redskins."

Both men laughed.

"Hell, let me get to the saloon and change into some riding clothes. Then we'll get out there and go build them signal fires. I could use some of that profit, right now."

4

A robin fluttered to the ground six-feet from Chief Running Bear as he sat outside his tipi high on the Republican River where it swept into the state of Nebraska. The robin eyed the quiet figure of the Indian, worked at some wild seed on the ground, then spotted the telltale signs of earth movement that signaled an earth worm rising to the top.

The robin waited, checking the man thing from time to time. The moment the worm pushed his head out of the ground, the robin struck, caught the worm in her beak, braced her feet and pulled until the three-inch worm came free of the hole. The bird held the worm in the center and flew off to her nest.

Chief Running Bear had watched the robin with interest. He had seen it happen many times. The robin would make a good Brulé warrior. She knew always to be watchful, she knew how to be patient and wait until the enemy was in the right position, and she attacked with deadly, single-minded purpose, then flew off quickly with the spoils.

The head of this band of Southern Brulé Sioux stood tall for an Indian, five-feet eight with heavy black hair now braided on each side. A livid purple scar dented his right cheek where a Pony Soldier bullet had come close to killing him. Dark eyes stared at the world past a prominent, hooked nose. He had lived through thirty-six winters.

Running Bear sat near his tipi, the largest in the band at the center of the camp. He had three wives and six children, but only two sons. His shield, lance and bow and arrows stood proudly just to the right of the tipi opening. They told the world that a warrior lived here, a man who took pride in his weapons.

They were there also to be immediately available in case of an attack. But no attack was anticipated. The Southern Brulé Sioux were not at war with any other Indian tribe, even though there were several different tribes in the general area. It was not like the old days when each group of families or bands stayed in its own area for hunting and camping.

The new summer camp was a good one. They could stay here for a month before the grazing would be gone for their ponies.

Here were berries and roots they could gather, and hunting was good.

For a moment Running Bear wished for the glory days when he was a small boy yearning to become a warrior. Things had seemed so simple then. Warriors rode out on thrilling raids against their long time enemies, returned with scalps and coups and tales of bravery and valor! The women gathered roots and berries and nuts, made jerky and pemmican from the buffalo, and life was gentle, easy and wonderful.

Now it seemed that everyone hunted the Indians, not the buffalo. The Pony Soldiers slashed at them. Some of the other tribes had gone to the dreaded reservations. Those who did not sign the white eyes' paper were called outlaws and renegades and the Pony Soldiers hunted them like wolves even though they were in the Brulé's traditional homelands and hunting grounds.

Nearly all of the chiefs who signed the treaty papers with the white eye chiefs and generals did not have any idea what the papers said, or what they required of them. They signed only when they were assured they would be given gifts from the great white leader in Washington. The chiefs believed that the gifts were just that, presents. A gift given does not tie the Indian to any agreement. A gift is a gift, not a payment.

A small bundle of energy scurried out of Running Bear's tipi flap, stopped at once, and looked around. The small girl's hair which shone with the color of the sun had been braided and now hung at both sides. A week ago she had been Megan Freening. Now she was called Little Sunflower and wore a simple breechclout and nothing else. Already her shoulders, chest and back were taking on a soft tan from the sunshine.

She saw Running Bear and hurried over to him.

"I want my clothes back," she said using her best smile. She had found during the past four days that her best smile helped her get what she wanted. But this time nothing happened. The big man didn't understand. It was the same way when they talked to her. She didn't know the words.

Little Sunflower sat beside the chief for a while. She knew he was the boss. There were three women who lived in the tipi with him and that confused her. One of them must be his wife, but she wasn't sure which one.

Two of the women were working a few yards away. They sat on the ground where they had staked down buffalo hides and were scraping them with sharp rocks and the blade of an axe. Little Sunflower moved over to see better.

Watching Woman, the oldest of the three women scraping the hides, smiled at Little Sunflower and handed her a small scraping rock. She said something in the language Little Sunflower didn't understand. Then she took the rock, placed the flat side down on the big skin in front of them, and scraped toward herself with it. Then she pointed at Little Sunflower and handed her the scraper.

She tried it, and Watching Woman nodded and clapped her hands. Little Sunflower smiled and did it again. Watching Woman said something soothing and smiled, then went back to her own scraping.

For half an hour, Little Sunflower scraped on the skin, taking pride in getting it just right so Watching Woman smiled and nodded. Then she was tired of scraping. She lay down the stone and stood, expecting one of the women to grab her by the ear and push her back in place the way her Aunt Emma would have done.

None of the Indian women seemed to notice as she left. Nobody yelled at her. She wandered down to the small creek where they had camped near the larger river. She sat and played in the water for a while, then took off the funny little soft leather shoes they had given her, and stood in the chilly water.

Two small Indian girls came, chattered at her a minute, then took off their breech-clouts and splashed naked in the water. They motioned for her to join them. Take off her only bit of clothing? Right there in front of everyone? But the other girls had. She found the way the breechclout was fastened and slid out of it and walked into the water. Soon the three were having a game of tag and splashing joyously.

After they tired, they ran to the grassy bank of the stream and lay in the warm sun, letting it dry and toast them. For a few moments, Little Sunflower felt totally happy. She missed her mother and father, but had no idea what had happened to them. She remembered her real name, Megan Freening, but nobody called her that.

She didn't understand. But Watching Woman had been gentle with her, fed her, gave her things, and held her tight the first two nights when she cried and couldn't go to sleep. For now she would just play with these people and wait for her daddy to come and find her. That was it! She was lost. Her daddy and mother would find her soon.

Running Bear faced the warm sun and

relaxed. He had heard bad news from one of the men on the raid. The Pony Soldiers who chased them had been led by Captain Two Guns. The thought of the name made Running Bear wince and rub his scarred cheek. Captain Two Guns was known throughout the plains. He was a dangerous and courageous leader of the swift Pony Soldiers. When he rode, the men with him could match a Brulé mile for mile, a hundred miles a day without a change of ponies.

He was a devil who knew where to find the camps, attacked without warning, and when he captured a camp, he obliterated everything in it, burning, smashing, rendering everything useless.

Captain Two Guns was the most feared Pony Soldier in the whole blue coated army.

Now he was here. Why?

Chief Running Bear had talked with the survivor of the attack on the three warriors. They should have left the white eye's buffalo and ridden like the wind with the captured horses. Some of his people were developing a taste for the strange creatures the white eyes raised and called cattle. He would discourage the use of this animal whenever possible

Captain Two Guns. He must be with the

other Pony Soldiers down at the village near the Smoky Hill River to the south. That was a long ride for the bluecoats. Running Bear sighed. It was not a long ride for a Brulé, or for Captain Two Guns. Why did he fight the Indians so hard?

The chief watched Little Sunflower splashing in the river. Her hair would darken with age, but it would always be obvious that she was not a Brulé. Still he wanted to raise her as one. She would have the best training he could give her. She would know everything any Brulé woman knew. He would raise her to be the number one wife of a future great chief.

He watched three hunters leaving the camp. There would be a spring buffalo hunt soon, not to provide winter food, but to re-supply staples: sinew for bowstrings, buffalo skins for tipis and for robes, and all the other vital parts of their livelihood that depended upon products from the entire buffalo's body.

As he thought of it, Running Bear looked forward to the fresh taste of buffalo meat.

He returned to the primary cause of his concern. There must be a gathering of all the bands and tribes of the Kansas plains. They must unite in one alliance and defeat the Pony Soldiers. They must burn every fort in the area of the Republican, Saline, Solomon and Smoky Rivers and all the way to the great Arkansas River.

It must be done. An alliance of all the tribes and renegades to do what they should have done long ago. They had to kill every blue coat in the whole area. Then they could take apart the railroad, tear up the rails, burn the stations. After that it would be simple to rout every white-eye on the buffalo plains and drive those alive back to the Missouri River!

Yes, it must be done.

Already he had made plans to go visit the other Southern Brulé bands. He was sure that they all would join in the fight. He would also visit the Cheyenne, Arapaho and Oglala and it must be a joint effort so they could overwhelm the puny forts.

If the forts had six-hundred men, he must attack with three thousand to smash the white eyes' army and send any survivors rushing back across the plains toward the muddy river.

The great plains were Indian lands, and must remain so forever!

Running Bear left his seat near his tipi and walked among the one hundred other tipis that spiked into the sky along the small creek that ran into the Republican River.

There were other bands within two days' ride.

For generations, the Brulé had lived with nature, had known not to bring too many ponies together because there would not be enough grass for them to graze. To overfeed on one patch of land would kill it for years. They kept their bands small enough to facilitate quick movements to fresh graze, better hunting, and away from danger areas of other tribes — and lately, of the white eye.

His people conserved the natural resources, never cutting more trees than could grow back in a year, never spoiling a good fishing stream, never using up all the wild onions, but leaving some to produce more for the next year. They were one with nature, not like the white eyes who wanted to dig up Mother Earth's hair, turn it over and plant new crops in her rich soil.

The white eyes would ruin the land in fifty years if they had control of it. This had happened in the lands to the far east where their great grandfathers had lived.

Running Bear stopped at a tipi where Large Hand had lived. He was one of the two warriors lost on the last raid. His two wives were both still weeping and moaning. Both had slashes on their arms and breasts. Now there was no man to hunt for their tipi. Large Hand's first wife would go back to her father's tipi and the second wife would move to her sister's tipi and be second wife to her husband.

The tipi itself would be saved until the next move. If there were a new marriage, the tipi would be given to the new family for a small compensation of ponies to the widows.

The chief moved on, knowing that if they could put together the great alliance and attack the Pony Soldiers, there would be many more widows. Better a few widows now than the Brulés be slaughtered like buffalo forced over a steep cliff. Better to fight and die than to perish like dumb animals unable to resist.

The next day Chief Running Bear would leave for his trip to talk to the Oglalas. He would take only one warrior with him so there could be no hint of pressure. First he hoped that he could find Swift Bird. He had met the chief before. Swift Bird was a man he could talk to and make plans with.

The more he walked, the more Running Bear became certain that the Pony Soldiers' settlement on the Smoky Hill was the key where they must strike first. It was on the Iron Horse railroad. There were two other forts on the rails, then one at the headwaters of the Smoky Hill River itself. When they had burned down all four of those clusters of buildings, and killed or routed the Pony Soldiers and the blue shirts on the ground, they would be in command of the entire area.

It had to be done, and done soon.

Back at Running Bear's big tipi, Little Sunflower had stood patiently while Waiting Woman had fitted the small dress over her. It was made of well chewed doeskin and was as soft and nice as any cloth she had ever seen.

"Dress," Waiting Woman said in the Sioux language, but Little Sunflower did not understand.

"*Miscunksi,* my daughter," Waiting Woman said. She repeated the word several times, pointing at the small girl with the golden hair. At last Little Sunshine repeated the word. The woman corrected her pronunciation, then beamed when the small girl said it again, correctly.

It was the start of a language lesson for the former Megan Freening that would last as long as she stayed with the Brulés.

"*Ina,*" the older woman said pointing to herself. She said it several times, and at last Little Sunflower said it three times and got the inflection exactly right. It was the

Lakotah word for mother, and Waiting Woman smiled and then went about her many tasks.

Chief Running Bear left the next morning with a favorite warrior named Big Feet and took a two day ride to the Oglala Sioux camp of Swift Bird. They were met at the first tipi and escorted to the chief's tent as visiting dignitaries.

Swift Bird came out at once when he heard they had two of their cousins as guests and greeted them properly.

"Welcome to the camp, cousins from the south. Welcome and come sit with us and talk and eat. Our camp is your camp."

The guests were shown inside the tipi, carefully went to the right and sat down only when Swift Bird suggested they sit. One of his wives brought bowls of stew from a pot hanging over the small cooking fire.

When they had eaten and the bowls taken away, Running Bear came to the point at once.

"The buffalo are being chased from their traditional feeding grounds by the white eyes. If we allow them to continue, the buffalo will be scattered and soon die out, and then all of the Plains Indians will die with them."

Swift Bird nodded. "We have seen the

Iron Horse and those who kill Mother Earth's hair and put up fences. They push the buffalo farther from us, disrupt his natural habits. Something must be done."

Quickly Running Bear told his cousin of his plan for a great alliance of Plains Indians to rid the land of the Pony Soldiers, then all white eyes.

Swift Bird sat back and nodded. He folded his arms over his chest and stared into the small fire.

"Many times we have talked of a great alliance. It has never happened. But you are right. We must unite, gather our forces and overrun the puny Pony Soldier forts. They are all made of wood and will burn like a thousand camp fires."

The Oglala Sioux medicine man had sat in on the talks and he said little but nodded his agreement.

After an hour of talk, Swift Bird called for his pipe. He filled it, lit it and puffed, then passed it to Running Bear and Big Feet. Both smoked the pipe indicating their agreement of what had been discussed.

"When do we gather?" Swift Bird asked.

"Soon. We need to contact the rest of the bands of all tribes. Can you see the rest of the Oglalas?"

Swift Bird said he could, as well as some

of the Northern Cheyennes in his area. They split up that section of western Kansas, and each chief vowed to contact every band in the region and gain their support.

"We will meet back here in ten days time and discuss our progress," Running Bear suggested. They agreed. The business done, Swift Bird took the visitors to the pony herd to show them his new war pony he had just finished training.

The animal was a swift little claybank that could turn with a press of a knee, stop, spin around and dash off in another direction.

The kinsmen stayed the night, then the next morning headed out toward Beaver Creek where Swift Bird said six or eight bands of Arapahoes had been camped a week ago.

Running Bear and Big Feet worked their way back to their own camp on the Republican six days later. They had commitments from all except one of the bands to join in the alliance. They had three days to rest before they took the result of their campaign back to Swift Bird to set up a time to come together and start their great war of annihilation against the white eyes.

That evening the band met in council around the fire. Each of the dozen members of the council listened to the idea of the alliance and the great war against the Pony Soldiers and all white eyes who had flooded into their hunting grounds. After Running Bear gave his explanation, each of the council members had the right to speak.

All but one did, and each warrior spoke in favor of the plan. Each pledged to follow whatever leader the war chiefs of all of the bands named.

"We are being pushed too far," War Eagle said. "The white eyes say one thing, do another. They say we should go to the place reserved for us. But if they send us there now, they can change their minds and send us into the desert or the rocky hills tomorrow. We must fight now for our lands, for the hunting grounds where our buffalo may roam and breed and supply us with our needs for the next one thousand winters!"

Every one of the council members smoked the pipe as it came around. Running Bear's band had backed his idea of an alliance.

That afternoon in his tipi, Running Bear rested and played with the golden child. It was not considered right for a warrior to talk with a girl child, let alone laugh and tumble on a bed and play games with her. Running Bear ordered the tipi flap lowered so no one would come in without an invitation. He called the child to him with motions and talked to her. Soon she must learn the Lakotah language.

"*Hinziwin*, little yellow haired girl. I am your *ahte*, your father. You will be safe and warm and well fed in my band. Your *ina*, mother, will help take care of you, comfort you, teach you to speak our language. She will show you what a good Brulé Sioux woman must know, and you will be good at it."

He set her down and put on her the small doeskin dress that had rows of trader beads on it. For just a moment his big arms went around her and he held her. Then he let go, and lay down on his raised bed and drew the buffalo robes around him. It had been a long trip and he was tired.

Through his fatigue, Running Bear smiled. He had started something that would insure the life of his band, of his tribe, for years to come. The alliance would work, it would scatter the white eyes and drive them forever from the buffalo plains!

5

Millicent Kane tapped the toe of her high button black shoe on the wooden floor in her brother's living room.

"I simply cannot stand by and watch these innocent people slaughtered like they were animals!" Millicent railed. Her long brown hair swung as she turned and stared at each of the six people in the room. Her wide set eyes snapped.

"These are God's creatures. They are human beings just like you and me. Would we slaughter Germans or Italians or Chinese just because we don't understand them? Of course not. The Indian has had a tremendously bad reputation because we have promoted it. We are stealing, *yes, I said stealing,* his land and the land of his father and of his father before him. The American Indian has lived here for three or four hundred years!

"We are trampling his rights and his lifestyle and his whole culture into the dust . . . just so we can move West, so we can grab his land and his natural resources and his timber and gold and whatever else he has of value that we can steal from him!"

Elijah Grundy had been nodding as she spoke. He was a giant of a man, the town blacksmith and Baptist preacher in the only church in town.

"Amen! Amen! Sister Millicent!" Grundy shouted. "Everything you say is true. That poor boy, Daylight, he was murdered, no doubt about that. We all know why, the Freening family. Yes, the Indians sometimes can be brutal and murdering — some of them. But some of our white people are that way, too. The problem is, Sister Millicent, what can we do about all this?"

"We can write our congressmen and our two senators," Millicent said at once. "Let them know how we feel. We're living right in the middle of this. We should have the say, not some old man in his Boston or New York living room!"

Sitting around the comfortable living room were the rest of the members of the Hays Benevolent Association. Lately they had been concentrating on helping out two poor families in town, but after the hanging, they had turned quickly to the Indian problem.

Two women were in the group besides

Millicent, along with Marshal Lloyd Menville, and Alonzo Croton. Alonzo was the richest man in town, and he was now building stock pens so Hays could become a center for shipping beef east on the Kansas Pacific Railroad all the way to Kansas City, and then on the Union Pacific into Chicago.

Alonzo watched the widow Kane. He was said to have a roving eye, and although married, was thought to be a womanizer. He lifted his heavy cane and shook his head.

"We must be cautious about this whole affair. The army has control over the Indians. Until they become citizens we can do little. We should be encouraging our senators to give these savages the responsibilities of citizenship. Then we could control them."

"Talk, talk, talk!" Millicent said sharply. "What are we going to do?"

"Write the letters," one of the women said.

The others nodded.

"Remember, Daylight was not a citizen in Hays or in Kansas," Marshal Menville said quickly. "I had no jurisdiction over him. But, I think we should write to the senators and tell them where we stand. If they get enough mail, it might do some good."

"Mr. Croton, will you write four letters to

Washington?" Millicent asked, smiling sweetly.

"Yes, Mrs. Kane, I will do that this afternoon," he said. He stared at her directly and at last she looked away.

"Thank you, Mr. Croton. I hope we all will write those letters. You know I asked the army at Fort Hays to send a representative here today to give the army viewpoint, but they said they had no one to send."

"Sounds normal," Croton said. He still watched Millicent.

"Our second big need is more members. I want each of you to bring one new member to the next meeting, which we've set for this same day next month. We'll see you all here . . . with your new member. Thank you for coming."

Juliana Bainbridge sat primly on the couch in her father's living room. It was early afternoon and her mother was having a short lay-me-down in her bedroom.

Lieutenant Ben Danalaw had slipped out of his duties with the Lightning troop and by arrangement met with Juliana. He sat beside her, his eyes glowing with devotion. "Juliana you're the prettiest little thing I ever have seen, all gussied up and soft and, golly, you even smell good."

Juliana, who had spent two hours getting ready for his visit, blushed prettily. "Lieutenant Danalaw, you say the nicest things. Sometimes I wonder if you mean it all."

"I mean it. I just can't think of enough beautiful things to say about you. Absolutely gorgeous: your long shining golden hair, beautiful lake blue eyes, high cheek bones that highlight a perfectly wonderful face. . . ."

Juliana smiled and leaned forward until her face was only inches from his. "You've never tried to kiss me, Ben."

"Oh . . . I . . . I didn't think you would let me."

"You won't know until you try."

He leaned in and their lips met in a quick kiss, then he jolted back.

"Oh, lord, Juliana! You don't know what that does to me."

She had hardly moved. He put his arms around her and kissed her again, harder this time, demanding. She returned some of the fire and then gently pulled away.

"Glory!" Ben said softly, "I . . . I guess this means that we're ready to get engaged to be married."

Juliana shook her head, her heart still thumping so hard in her chest she could hardly understand him. At last it came through.

"No, Ben, I'm not even thinking about getting engaged." She smiled. "But so you won't be so disappointed. . . ."

She reached for him and pulled his face down to hers, kissing him hotly this time. His hand slipped up and fondled her breasts. It was a moment before she realized what his hand was doing. She stepped back, shook her head.

"No, Ben!" she hissed. "If mother caught you doing that you'd never get in the front door again."

"But, Juliana," he whispered. "You make me so . . . so hot! I want you so much. Do you understand?"

"That's married talk, Ben. Since we're not married, you stop talking that way, or I won't let you in the door. Now be nice. Just cool down. Is the picnic all planned? I'll wear something that will dry off quickly after we splash."

"Yes, all planned."

Ben Danalaw made up his mind right then. She was a fine woman. She wasn't easy, she had stopped him firmly but gently. She was the woman he was going to marry. Juliana didn't realize it yet, but he would make her fall in love with him. The sooner the better.

Juliana teased Ben for five minutes more, then insisted that he leave before her mother got up from her nap. He reluctantly agreed.

Later that afternoon Juliana watched the horseback troops work on their drills. She stood near where the Lightning troop paraded through the formations that were supposed to make them better riders, more alert and quicker responding to commands in an engagement with the hostiles.

As Juliana watched, Dr. Constatine walked up beside her and tipped his hat.

"Afternoon, Miss Juliana. Enjoying some air?"

"No, I'm watching the drill. I think Lieutenant Danalaw is just so handsome on his mount, ordering the troop around that way."

Dr. Constatine watched them a moment. He'd seen a lot of cavalry troops and this one's skill was far below average.

"What about that Lieutenant Turnball? I hear you think he's pretty nice, too."

"Oh, yes, of course. I just haven't made up my mind between them. After all, I'm not really an old maid until I'm nineteen," she laughed.

"True, Juliana. I just want to caution you

a little. Men get all riled up where a pretty girl is the prize. Back in Chicago I had to treat a young man who got into a duel over a girl on the post. He had a gunshot wound just over his heart. He lived but spent three months in the hospital. Then he and the other officer were both retired from the service."

Captain Constatine watched Juliana closely.

"All I'm saying is I sure don't want that to happen here. Don't push this rivalry between our officers too far."

Juliana's pretty face changed gradually into an angry frown.

"Captain, why don't you just mind your own business? You have no call to scold me that way. I'll do what I want to do, when I want to do it. You just tend to your old pills and potions."

Juliana turned and flounced back toward the officer quarters.

Doctor Constatine watched her go and shook his head sadly. "Damn," he said softly to no one in particular. "Damn, but that little wench is going to cause trouble. I can feel it."

Juliana looked over her shoulder at Dr. Constatine once as she pranced back to her father's quarters. Why was the captain being so mean to her? He didn't have the right to scold her. She was just having fun with the two lieutenants. They were the only two choices. The captains were already married.

She slipped inside the house to find her mother singing softly to herself and dusting the parlor.

"Have a nice walk, dear?" Mrs. Bainbridge asked.

"Yes, but I'm a little tired. I think I'll lie down a while before supper. Call me if you want me to help you."

Her mother smiled at her and Juliana went into her own bedroom. It was a nice enough room, but she liked their quarters much better when they had been stationed at the army headquarters in Chicago. Besides, there were a lot more officers there, and even some boys her own age.

She hurried into her room, slid the bolt on the door quietly and sprawled on the bed.

Chicago. She remembered Billy the most. Now she couldn't even think of his last name. He had been about six months older than she. He was fun to talk to and quite attractive, too. They had been friends for six months or so, and then one day in the summer they were in her parents' quarters and her mother had to go to the neighbors. As soon as the door closed, Billy had hurried up to Juliana and grabbed her roughly and kissed her.

"I never kissed a girl with such big . . . with such developed . . ."

"Breasts," Juliana filled in for him and giggled.

"Yeah," Bill said. Then he kissed her again.

Juliana rolled over on the bed and on her back and one hand trailed over her breasts. That had been the first time a boy had ever touched her . . . there. He had kissed her twice more and she thought the world was going to melt. She felt warm all over and wanted him to kiss her forever.

Then before she knew it, his hands were on her breasts, rubbing. It had felt so good! Quickly he pushed his hand between buttons and under her chemise and grasped her bare breast rubbing tenderly.

It had almost been too much for her. She felt tears coming down her cheeks, and then he kissed them away. He bent and kissed her breast through the dress. She knew she was going to explode. Her nipple was hot and tight and she wanted to scream in joy!

Billy had taken her hand and put it on his crotch where a large, long lump had grown.

Now as Juliana thought about it, she could feel her breasts getting warm. Her hand rubbed them gently, then harder. She opened her dress top and pushed her hand inside on her bare breasts and petted herself. It felt so good!

A moment later her other hand slipped down to her crotch and pulled up her long skirt. Her hand rubbed the soft place gently, and she felt the thrill, the surge of hot blood all through her body. Then someone knocked on the door.

"Juliana, I need some flour. Could you run down to the cutler's store and buy five pounds for us? Right away, Juliana. I need it to make supper."

"Yes, mama. Just let me wake up a little bit. I'll be right there."

Juliana frowned and shook her head, buttoned up her blouse and adjusted it. She slid open the bolt without a sound and went in and talked to her mother. Then she hurried down to the store on the post where the troops and officers could buy things they needed that weren't issued to them.

Juliana breathed deeply and by the time she got to the small store, she was almost back to normal. The flush was gone from her cheeks. She bought the flour and some horehound candy, then headed back home.

All the way she tried to figure out how she could get R. J. Turnball to be more romantic. He never had even thought about kissing her. He had come courting twice, but they only sat and talked. Sunday after next he would show her how to play bridge. But that was too far off. She needed something quicker. Somehow she had to trick or tease him into kissing her.

Then he would think that he, too, would have a real chance with her. Who knows, he might propose first, even before Ben Danalaw.

Which one did she like the best? So far Ben was by far the best kisser, and he had fondled her breasts. Ben was definitely ahead so far.

Juliana smiled and hurried back home. She would figure out something to attract Lieutenant Turnball. She would get it all worked out before she went to sleep tonight!

On the parade ground, Lieutenant Danalaw worked his troop hard. He had only thirty-five men at the present time, but he had spoken to Colonel Harding and they had an appointment right after supper to check over the troop and work out a new training schedule.

He raced down the line of troopers.

"No, No, No! Bilstrap. Don't you know how to ride a horse? Damn! Sergeant

Ivanar, take this man, and anyone else who can't even ride, and put them through a special training course. Start at the beginning with saddling, care, leading, walking and riding. These men will have an extra hour of drill before any chow. Move them out now, you know damn well who they are!"

"Yes sir, Lieutenant. Bilstrap, fall out and follow me."

He went down the troop front picking out men he knew were not up to par for normal cavalry operations. He took seven men.

Lieutenant Danalaw scowled. That many? He was going to catch hell from Colonel Harding tonight. He knew the man was in headquarters probably watching the drill with binoculars. Tonight Danalaw knew he would get chewed out royally. He could take it if the Colonel had a good way to train the men, to get some spirit in them, and turn them into a potent, quick strike fighting force.

As Lieutenant Danalaw put his troops through a final troop front drill, he looked up to see a rider coming toward him.

"Oh, damn, Colonel Harding," he muttered.

He gave his troops a halt and rode up to meet the colonel. "Lieutenant Danalaw, Lightning Troop, reporting, sir."

Colt returned the salute. "At ease, Lieutenant. Looks like we've got our work cut out for us."

"Yes sir. A few of my men can't even ride."

"I see you're working on that."

"Yes sir."

"Good. Put the troop into a column of fours and then another troop front. I'd like to watch it from close up."

"Yes sir." Lieutenant Danalaw saluted, swung his mount around and rode back to his men.

Colt watched as the troops maneuvered. The cavalry usually moved from one spot to another in a column four abreast. That's no formation from which to engage an enemy, however. There were various formations to move into from the column of fours. One of the best was a troop front which put every horse in line shoulder to shoulder ready to advance.

Colt watched the maneuver, told Lieutenant Danalaw to put the men back into a column of fours so he could talk to them. They soon were in position.

He rode midway along the ranks and turned toward them.

"Men, you're in a Lightning unit because you volunteered. It's going to be tough duty from here on. You'll work your asses off, but it will mean something.

"You stick with Lightning Troop and you'll be the best damn trained soldiers in the U.S. Army, bar none! You'll get more time on the target range than the rest of the men in the fort combined. And you'll learn to use your horse to its ultimate ability and value to you as a fighting man.

"Lieutenant Danalaw, after I've left put the men in a company front again."

"Yes sir."

"I'm going to put on a quick little demonstration. I want you all to watch carefully, because to remain in the Lightning Troop, each one of you is going to have to ride past a stationary target doing what I'm going to do and hit that target twice out of five rounds."

Colt pulled his mount's head around and galloped fifty yards down from the troopers. He hooked the toe of his left boot into the left stirrup, slid off the right side of the horse until the stirrup lifted to the top of the saddle and held firm. He slapped the mount to get it galloping back the way he had come, leaned down and held the saddle horn with his left hand. Now he could swing his body forward and look under the neck of the horse. He urged the mount to a faster gallop. Then, as he came along the troopers, he fired his pistol at the men six times. He spaced the shots from one end of the line of twenty-five cavalrymen to the other.

Then he pulled himself up into the saddle and rode back to where the troopers were in a state of shock.

Lieutenant Danalaw got to him first.

"Sir, how in hell. . . . You looked like a damn Indian, the way they ride off the horse that way and shoot their bows. . . ."

Colt grinned at Lieutenant Danalaw and motioned for them to ride back to the troops. He moved to the center of the ranks and called for them to move in around him.

When the chatter quieted down he tossed them a question.

"Troopers, do you think you can fire under your mount's neck that way and hit what you aim at?"

A chorus of "no's" came to him with a few positive notes.

"You can. Any man who can fork a horse can do what I just did . . . but it will take some training, some know-how and a lot of practice. How many of you have been in an Indian fight and had the savages come at you that way?"

A dozen men held up their hands.

"It doesn't leave much of a target for you,

does it? We do the same thing right back at them. Oh, by the way, I was using blanks that I fixed up just before I came out. The only thing you could have been hit with was some paper wadding."

The men laughed.

"You laugh now, but most of you were ducking."

He watched the men. Most of them seemed to enjoy his little trick.

"We'll see how much you enjoy ducking the real thing tomorrow. Colonel Adamson has authorized a five day patrol. We'll hear Boots and Saddles at 4:45 A.M. and be out of the fort by 5:00. We'll be traveling light. No sabers, one blanket, no bugle, no tents, bring one change of socks. Your sergeants will relay other particulars.

"Oh, yes, you will draw three days' rations. Three days' rations for a five day trip. Think about that overnight."

He turned to Lieutenant Danalaw. "Dismiss your troop, and report to me in the Commander's office for further instructions."

They exchanged salutes and Colt rode back to the fort commander's office where his orderly took his horse.

Lieutenant Danalaw was in the door a minute behind him.

"Sir, a trial by fire?"

"Best kind, Lieutenant. Do you object?"

"No sir. But some of the men might not be able to make it."

"This is a good way to find out. We will do little that any normal cavalryman can't or hasn't done. It will be stretching their capabilities only a little."

He reached to the desk he had been provided and picked up a sheet of paper.

"Here's a list of equipment for each man. How many of your troopers have Spencer rifles?"

"Only the non-coms and myself."

"Report to the quartermaster officer and exchange any he has in stock for the breech loaders. Eventually all of your troop will carry the Spencer. Have an impromptu class tonight by the sergeants for anyone getting the new weapon. I want them to be able to use them if we need them."

"Yes sir. I doubt if Lieutenant Paulson has more than five or six in stock. It's a popular piece."

"Tomorrow we're going to head out on a quick survey of hostiles and see how many summer camps we can find. We won't plan on attacking any of them this time out. We'll have the best trackers with us and a good map man who will generate a map as we move. We probably won't go out more than a hundred miles or so."

"Yes sir. There's one point I'm curious about. The rations, sir?"

"Puzzles you, eh, Lieutenant? Good. You think on it. But be sure each man draws only three days of rations. I'll see you here in the morning promptly at 4:30 A.M. for a final briefing."

"Yes sir."

Lieutenant Danalaw saluted smartly, did a snappy about face and hurried out the door with the equipment list. He'd never been on a patrol with such a meager list of equipment. And no tent, not even for the officers. Just what the hell had he got himself into with this Lightning company?

Then he remembered the way that light colonel had slid to the side of his mount, galloped by and fired six blanks at them from under the horse's neck. Damn, *he* was going to have to learn to do that.

Lieutenant Danalaw broke into a grin as he pushed open the barracks door and hurried in to talk to his Lightning troop sergeants.

6

It was still early morning when the Lightning Troop with Lieutenant Danalaw and Colonel Harding in command crossed the Saline River north of the village of Hays, Kansas, and rode on a northwest route heading for the south fork of the Solomon River.

Colt had moved the troop out smartly at a walk designed to cover four miles per hour. After the first half hour when the animals were well warmed up, he moved them into a canter, a natural gait for the mounts. The canter was how the troops could cover six to eight miles per hour depending on how Colt pushed them.

Most of the troopers were surprised by the cantering. Colt moved up and down the column of fours looking for the men's reaction. No officer had ever asked most of them what they thought about an army move. They appreciated it. A few were too flustered to respond. Some of the enlisted men had never spoken to an officer over the rank of lieutenant before. Most enjoyed the faster pace.

Colt had also brought along his six Pawnee scouts. The lead scout, Short Grass, had been briefed by Colt the night before and was told to bring his best hunters. Tracking would probably not be used at all. Short Grass had simply nodded and walked away.

That morning, he and his five men waited at the fort commander's office. Short Grass wore an army hat and blue blouse. The rest of the scouts had no official clothing. Two had civilian trousers. Only two of the others wore shirts. It was summer! Colt put Short Grass in front of the troop, told him to maintain a mile interval and to report back if he spotted any Indian summer camps.

A second scout held a position a quarter-of-a-mile ahead of the main body as a connecting file.

This morning Colt took the lead and placed Lieutenant Danalaw half way along the column. Beside Colt rode Corporal Harley Otto who had an unofficial reputation as being quite an artist.

He carried two foot square pads of paper in his saddlebags and now held another as they rode. He had a dozen pencils all carefully knife-sharpened and ready for use.

"Sir, you want me to do a map as we ride?"

"Right, Corporal Otto. Do it rough as we move and when we take a break you can use your notes to do a better rendering of it before you forget the details. I want it done in sections so we can glue them together once we get back to the fort and have a detailed map of this area. Put down landmarks, recognition points, dead snags, bends in the river, bluffs, sand hills and so on.

"I know the distances and miles will be estimated, but we'll do the best we can."

"Yes sir. I'll enjoy doing it. Do I have permission to leave the formation now and again to sketch something I want to remember, perhaps work on my rough map?"

"If you need to. Check out with Sergeant Ivanar, and never get more than a hundred yards behind the end of the troop."

"Yes sir!"

The other four scouts were sent out with their bows and arrows to hunt up a noon meal. They were clearly instructed not to use their fire arms in hunting.

At the first sighting of the South Fork of the Solomon River, Colt turned his troops hard west. They rode until noon working the ground-eating canter. When the sun was directly overhead, Short Grass and his four hunters appeared in a thick tangle of brush and cottonwoods in a small valley a mile from the Solomon.

Colt looked over the results of the hunt. Four partridge, eight large rabbits, and six Chinese pheasants.

The surprising order went out quietly:

"Troops, cool out your horses and picket them in the best grass you can find. We'll be here for six or seven hours."

Colt asked the Pawnee to cook the meat. Two Indians began gathering dead, dry wood from the patch of cottonwoods. They used two short shovels that had been brought along to dig a trench six feet long and a foot wide and a foot deep.

In the trench they built their fire, stretching it out the length of the digging. The fire was made of dry wood. Colonel Harding ordered the men to come and watch.

"Look at the wood they use. It's dead and dry as an old maid. Look at the fire, practically no smoke. We don't want to notify the hostiles that we're in the area. Now, watch closely what these Pawnees do. By the time your training is over you'll each have to gather wood and make a smokeless fire. Remember, it could save your scalp someday."

When the fire had burned down to glowing coals, the Pawnee brought in the birds and rabbits. Each had been coated with a thick layer of mud from the nearby small stream. The troopers stared in amazement.

"Hey, thought we was gonna get to eat them birds," one trooper called.

"Watch," Colt said.

The birds and rabbits were placed in the trench directly on top of the coals, then the dirt dug from the trench scooped quickly over the mud caked birds and the fire. Soon nothing could be seen of the food or the coals.

"In about a half hour, your noon day dinner will be ready," Colt said. "Until then I want every man to clean his weapon, tend to his mount and make sure he's ready for a fire fight. We have guards out, but in hostile country we have to be ready to fight at any time."

The dinner was a smashing success. The men ate some of the hardtack biscuits they had brought and each had half a bird or rabbit. It was more than most of them could eat, but the meat would not save over until the next day cooked or raw.

There were twenty-five troopers, including Lieutenant Danalaw. With the six Pawnees and Colt they had a total of thirty-two guns. He hoped they didn't blunder into a

force of two or three hundred hostiles looking for a fight.

Lieutenant Danalaw had chosen a pheasant to eat and now put down the rest of it.
"More than I usually consume," he said.

"In the field with the Lightning Troop,
you eat and sleep all you can, when you can.
No telling when we'll get much of either one
again."

Lieutenant Danalaw lifted his brows,
took a drink from his battered metal cup
and dug into the last drumstick and wing
from the pheasant.

Colt finished his half a rabbit and leaned
back. Lieutenant Danalaw stared at him
where they sat beside the small trickle of
water.

"Sir, could I ask why we're going to be
here so long?"

"Simple, Danalaw. This is a reconnaissance patrol. We're looking for everything
we can see and record. We have no desire to
let our presence be known to the hostiles.
That's why most of our movement will be
by night, starting with darkness tonight. As
soon as the men finish eating I want you to
order them to lay down and rest, sleep if
they can.

"Tell them we'll be riding most of the
night, until four A.M. at least. They either

sleep now or wait until daylight tomorrow."

"Yes sir, I'll put out the order. We've been riding almost seven hours. That's more than a good day's ride for most cavalry outfits. I think they'll be tired enough to sleep."

"Danalaw, we're in hostile territory. I want you to maintain alert guards, at least six of them. Cover every side. The scouts will also pull guard duty."

The young officer started to salute, but a frown from Colt stopped him.

"Yes sir, I'm sorry. No saluting in the field. No better way to tell the enemy who to shoot first that way. I'll get the troop settled down." He scurried away and Colt smiled. The young man from West Point might make a good Lightning Troop leader yet.

That night at dusk they pulled out of the woods and angled north toward the southern fork of the Solomon River.

Colt called the artist, who had detailed a foot square map of their journey so far. It was clear, well done, and would be a valuable addition to the fort's maps. This one showed ridges, small valleys, and rivers and even streams draining into them.

Colt turned the page and found a drawing of the Pawnee making the fire pit. It showed the pit being dug on one end and the rabbits going in on the coals on the other and being covered with dirt.

"Good work," Colt said. "How come you're in the army?"

"It's impossible for a young artist to make a living on the outside, sir. I'm doing sketch pads full of pictures about the army. Maybe I can have them published someday, or open up a gallery in Washington near army headquarters."

"Good idea," Colt said. "That will be the closest thing most of those headquarters soldiers get to an Indian campaign."

Colt put the sketches away as the light faded, took the lead and sent out his two scouts. Now they would really start their work.

When they hit the Southern Fork of the Solomon, they turned upstream. After three miles of silent riding, they found an Indian village nestled among some cottonwoods and willow. Colt had Lieutenant Danalaw count the tipis.

They circled around the camp and moved on upstream. Colt told Corporal Otto to make a note of the camp and to show the figure 64 at the spot for 64 tipis.

"Does that mean sixty-four warriors in that camp as well?" Corporal Otto asked.

"Roughly. We don't want to go in and

count red noses, however, do we, corporal?"

"No sir!"

By midnight they had found no new camps. The Southern Fork of the Solomon extended more than a hundred and fifteen miles westward from Fort Hays. Which meant they had a long way to go to check out all of the stream. They wouldn't get it done today. Colt called a halt shortly after midnight to give the horses and the men a rest.

The stream had shrunk dramatically. Another ten or twelve miles could be all they would need to search. If the stream grew too small, it could not support a band of Indians of any size. Most horses need ten to fifteen gallons of water a day to stay healthy. A small stream could not support a herd of two or three hundred horses.

The men were told to munch on hardtack and salt pork for their cold midnight meal. Most were still filled with the feast of wild meat that noon, and confined their snacking to hardtack and some bread some of them had come up with before they left the fort.

Colt found a sheltered place and lit a candle for Corporal Otto so he could finish his mapping. Colt also studied his own map of the area he had sketched from the one on the commander's wall.

He decided the stream would be followed for another two hours, perhaps three, then they would move north hoping to cross the Bow River, a middle fork on the Solomon.

A half hour later the troops were mounted up and the soft commands given to ride ahead. Less than two miles ahead they found another sleeping Indian village. Colt had no way of telling what band or from which tribe the hostiles might hail. They swung past after counting 46 tipis, and moved on upstream on the Southern Fork of the Solomon.

When the stream dwindled to six feet across and less than a foot deep, Colt called a halt. It was almost three A.M. The men tended to their horses, wiping them down, giving them a handful of oats and then picketing them in a grassy meadow. The men bedded down on their single blankets under a small stand of hardwood trees of a half dozen different species that Colt didn't recognize.

Four men guarded, and changed every two hours. The hunters were out all day. Colt and Short Grass made a quick scouting mission at daylight, staying in the trees and brush most of the time. They angled north for six miles, found what they thought was the headwaters of the Bow River and retreated without seeing any hostiles.

Colt checked the four daytime guards, then slept beside his saddlebags for four hours. He was up when the hunters got in at four in the afternoon. He told Short Grass to have them cook any fresh meat the same way they did the day before. The Pawnees had found only rabbits this day, but they were larger with much more meat on them. The eight rabbits would feed the entire troop.

Colt stared out from a small rise toward the north. Lieutenant Danalaw pushed in beside him.

"We moving north tonight?" Danalaw asked.

"Yes. Short Grass and I found what we think is the Bow. We'll try to cover both the Bow and the North Fork of the Solomon on the same sweep. They are never more than ten or twelve miles apart here. We'll split up and each go down one river. You'll have Short Grass with you on the Bow and I'll take the North Fork."

"How do we get back together?"

"The two run together. First one who gets to the juncture waits for the other, out of sight, of course."

"We count tipis and avoid contact with

127

the savages, right?"

"Absolutely. Unless you want to use fifteen men to take on a whole village with maybe sixty or seventy outraged Sioux or Cheyenne warriors."

"I'll pass on that."

"Better."

Colt kept looking north. He had not seen a single wisp of smoke anywhere in a 180 degree view. "There must be twenty bands of Indians out there somewhere. Probably twelve hundred warriors. Why have we found only two villages?"

"Looking in the wrong place. Must be to the west along the Beaver, Sappa and Prairie Dog Rivers."

"I hope so. Not sure we'll have time to check them all out. By the time we get to the juncture of the Bow and the North Fork, we'll be back to almost due north of Fort Hays. Might be the smart move to just turn south and head to our base."

· "We've been out two days," Lieutenant Danalaw said, thinking out loud. "Another two days to get to the juncture, I'd guess. That would put us at five days back to Fort Hays."

"True. We'll play it day by day."

The sun dropped below the horizon and darkness came quickly.

"Let's get saddled up," Colt said brusquely.

They moved out five minutes later.

They found the Bow River an hour later, moved down it a half mile to make sure. Then Colt let Lieutenant Danalaw split his command. Colt took half, and Sergeant Ivanar, and three scouts, and headed north to find the North Fork of the Solomon.

It was right where Colt figured it would be. He had brought along Corporal Otto, who was getting good at making sketches in the dark. They checked the river for a mile upstream. It was considerably larger than the South Fork had been, but they found no signs of camps. They retraced their steps and moved along the river cautiously.

Half a mile down they found the first camp. Working around it silently they counted 80 tipis. Two miles farther down they found another village comprised of 45 tipis. Colt asked one scout to walk into the camp and try to identify which tribe it might be.

He came back quickly.

"Cheyenne," the Pawnee scout said shortly. "Shields and long lances — Cheyenne."

They moved again, quietly, swiftly. This time it was five miles to the next camp, one with more than 100 tipis scattered along the river. Again the same scout called Small Deer, said they were Northern Cheyenne.

They moved another ten miles without finding a new camp, and Colt relaxed a little. He checked his pocket watch inside a fold of his blanket with a match for light. It was after three A.M. He sent Small Deer out to find a good spot to hide out during the day.

They had traveled another mile down the North Fork of the Solomon when Small Deer met them. He pointed south. They rode two miles into a thick stand of cottonwood and hickory that they had trouble riding into. It was perfect cover.

The troops and Colt ate cold rations and then went to sleep on the cold ground. Colt felt his rheumatism kicking up. It always did after two or three nights sleeping on the ground. Almost every man in the army had the ailment to some degree. It was one of the hazards of army life. He told the guard to wake him at daylight and went to sleep.

Colt came awake suddenly. Someone had shaken his shoulder.

"Quiet, sir, we have company," Sergeant Ivanar whispered. "Three hunters. The scouts said they are Arapaho."

Colt came up from his blanket and adjusted his two pearl handled pistols. He moved forward to the edge of the thicket and saw the red men working silently through some light brush to the north. It was daylight.

One Arapaho shot an arrow and scurried up and lifted high a rabbit. He tied it over his shoulder on rawhide and swung away from their cover. The two other hunters were farther away, but they, too, now moved to the north.

Colt watched them until they were out of sight.

"Arapaho," Small Deer said. He had slid to the ground beside Colt without making a sound.

"Their village four miles downstream," Small Deer said. "Saw sign last night."

Colt let only two of the three scouts go out hunting for their evening meal. He made sure they moved farther to the south, away from the Arapaho camp.

Colt slept in fits and starts through the rest of the day. He was running on about half the sleep he usually needed. By four that afternoon the hunters came back with two twenty-pound wild turkeys. The birds were too big to roast whole inside a mud pack and buried in the coals.

Colt had the turkeys scalded with hot water, the feathers picked off them, then let the men cut up the birds and cook them on sticks over the smokeless fires the Pawnee kept going. Before dusk the men had eaten more than they should have.

Colt knew he didn't want to look another turkey drumstick in the face for at least two months. As soon as it was dark they mounted up and moved back toward the North Fork.

That night they found three more camps. Colt counted and estimated the number of tipis. There were 45 in the first, 60 in the second and about 40 in the third.

They met Lieutenant Danalaw near where the Bow joined the flow of the North Fork just before dawn and moved together twelve miles to the South Fork of the Solomon and found a good place to hide out during the day.

Colt and Lieutenant Danalaw compared their finds.

"We could scare up only two bands in summer camps on the Bow," Danalaw said. "We figured 50 tipis in the first and 40 in the second. Short Grass said they were Arapaho."

Both officers agreed that their men were in good shape. They had been fed well, still had the bulk of their army rations, and after six hours of sleep would be rested.

"We'll sleep now and move out at twelve noon. With any luck we'll be able to sleep in our own bunks tonight."

They pushed off from their cover just after twelve noon and made good time. The men were anxious to get back to their warm bunks and off the cold ground. Colt pushed them into an eight miles per hour pace for two hours, then dropped it to six as the men and animals began to tire. He called a halt after three hours for a meal of army rations.

Soon they moved again. The countryside was more level here, gently rolling with occasional flat stretches of a dozen miles or more.

About six o'clock Colt figured they were not more than twenty miles north of the Fort. The Sabine River would be showing soon. They came over a small rise in the undulating short grasses of the prairie and saw smoke.

The angry plume grew as it lifted over a slight rise to the right. The smoke was dark and angry.

"That's no prairie grass fire," Colt called. The black smoke told him it was buildings and roofing and perhaps some oil or leather as well.

He moved the troop out at a gallop for

half a mile to a point where they could see the fire. As they did they could hear an occasional rifle shot.

Colt trained his binoculars on the small ranch.

"Indian raiders!" he bellowed, and led the men down the slight slope at a gallop toward the ranch a quarter of a mile away. Colt brought out his Spencer and fired all seven shots in the direction of the ranch to attract the savages' attention.

"Must be a dozen or more hostiles," Lieutenant Danalaw shouted as they galloped forward.

"Bring the men into a troop front!" Colt called.

Lieutenant Danalaw repeated the order and the column of fours spread out in orderly fashion just like on the parade field, only this was a real fight.

"Hold your fire for my command!" Colt bellowed. Lieutenant Danalaw and each sergeant and corporal along the line of thirty charging horses and men repeated the order.

The gunfire at the ranch stopped. Colt saw the savages looking their way, then they broke and raced away to the west.

Colt quickly ordered Lieutenant Danalaw to take half the troop to the ranch and offer any assistance possible. He took the second half of the troop and angled toward the savages, cutting them off, forcing them to ride farther south or be intercepted.

Colt had reloaded his Spencer with a new tube of rounds through the stock and now leveled in and fired three rounds at the fleeing dozen warriors.

"Fire at will!" Colt shouted. The troopers responded with a ragged volley of fire that then continued as they loaded and locked each round in the breech loaders.

One hostile spilled from his horse and didn't move. As they closed on the fleeing savages, a horse went down and the Indian scrambled for cover.

Sergeant Ivanar took two troopers and rode the Indian down, killing him with three rounds before they continued the chase.

Colt's big black gelding responded to the race and gradually outdistanced the rest of the troopers. He closed on the last Indian who now had only a bow and arrow. Colt used the Spencer and in spite of the uneven, jolting ride, got off three shots. The last one ripped through the Indian's back and blew him off his mount.

Two of the hostiles turned and fired with rifles, but missed, and Colt cut down another one. Nine savages fled the scene of their raid, but not before Colt emptied one of his pearl handled revolvers at them.

He held up his hand, stopping the chase. He checked his men. One had been hit in the shoulder but still held his seat. Another trooper stopped the bleeding and put on a makeshift bandage.

When the horses had a ten minute blow, Colt turned them back to the ranch at a walk.

After they covered the two miles to the ranch buildings, they saw that the fire in the house had been put out with a bucket brigade from the well. The fire had only started when Colt's men raced in.

The barn was burning itself out, nothing could save it.

Colt met Lieutenant Danalaw and stepped down from his saddle.

"Sir, this is the Shipley family. They've been here six years and never been attacked before. They think they were Brulé Sioux. The Shipleys lost two dead, a teenage son and a ranch hand who got caught in the open."

Dusk crept over the prairie.

"Tell the Shipleys that we'll camp here tonight and keep out guards in case the hostiles try to return. The men are to stay clear of the family, eat their army rations, and stand by for guard duty. Put six guards out on the perimeter. Change them every two hours."

Colt Harding went up to the house, his army hat in his hand.

A middle-aged rancher with a weathered face and a hat line showing at the middle of his forehead where no tan could be seen, came to the door before Colt could knock.

"Want to thank you, Colonel. They had us on the run. Blamed savages had rifles. Must have been three or four. Them damned flaming arrows would have done us in right soon. Oh, my name's Ted Shipley. This is my spread, the Circle S. Not big, but we're growing. Were growing, that is."

"I'm sorry about this, Mr. Shipley." Colt shook the man's hand and nodded toward the house. "You have any wounded?"

"Nope, just two dead. We'll bury them tomorrow. Lost my oldest son." The man turned away. "A body never counts on out-living his offspring. Just don't seem right somehow."

He turned back, the emotion controlled.

"Reckon we'll be having supper sometime soon. You welcome to join us. We owe you and your men more than we can ever pay."

"Thank you, but I'll eat army chow with the men. We'll camp here tonight and have out guards in case the hostiles try to come back. We punished them enough so I think they'll keep running."

"You kill any of the bastards?"

"Four of them that we know of, Mr. Shipley."

"That's some consolation. My wife and I thank you again."

Colt nodded and went back to his troopers. They had spread themselves out along a thin creek line. The horses had been rubbed down, fed a handful of oats and were working on some grass.

Colt settled down on his blanket and munched some hardtack. It was supposed to keep you alive, but he always had doubted that a trooper could live on army field rations for long and keep on riding and fighting.

Lieutenant Danalaw came up. "Sir, the guards are posted and the sergeant has a list for rotation."

"Good, Danalaw. Get some sleep. We'll have a late start in the morning. We should be to the fort before midday."

The nine remaining Brulés rode far into the night. They soon realized that the Pony

Soldiers were not following them. They made circles and back tracked, rode in small streams and split up into nine trails to confuse anyone trying to track them.

About midnight they came back together, crossed the South Fork of the Solomon and only then let their horses rest.

Quiet Fox knew there would be much anger with them for not stopping to bring back their dead warriors. But the devil Pony Soldiers were everywhere! He had seen Captain Two Guns chasing them on a huge charger that seemed to breathe fire and eat up the Kansas plains in giant strides. They had been lucky to get away with their lives. There had been no chance at all to bring back their fallen warriors.

Quiet Fox talked to the other Brulés, and all but one confirmed that they had seen Captain Two Guns firing at them with his magic pistols. One man claimed the small gun had sent a slug slamming past him from three long arrow shots. It was an impossible range. The short guns were wonders.

The raiding party had not intended to go so far, but the ranch they had planned to raid was empty, abandoned, so they had pushed farther south.

When they arrived back at Running Bear's summer camp on the Republican

River two days later, they were exhausted, hungry and ill tempered.

Quiet Fox reported to Running Bear the fate of the raid, their losses, and the attack by Captain Two Guns.

"How is it possible that he can be everywhere?" Running Bear asked.

But he knew that the Pony Soldier devil was in the Smoky Hill fort. That was not a day's ride from where the raiders were hit. He questioned Quiet Fox about the lost warriors, and indicated that it was Quiet Fox's job to explain to the grieving widows why their husbands would not be given a proper burial.

Running Bear waved the warrior away, then closed the tipi flap and ate from the stew Waiting Woman had prepared from several kinds of roots, wild onions and a rabbit. When he finished, he called Little Sunflower to him.

They sat down on his bed and he talked to her in Lakotah. She must learn the language of The People.

"You will grow and learn and someday you will be a proper Brulé wife for a great Sioux chief. I will be proud of you and you will have many children, all sons, who will grow and know both camps and be able to talk to the white eyes and with the Brulés and Oglalas and Cheyennes, and will help our people to win their wars and maintain our position here on the great plains which the buffalo call home."

Megan Freening looked up at the large Indian not understanding a word he said. Suddenly she felt lonely. She wanted to go back to her family, her mother and father and her two sisters. Where were they? Why hadn't her daddy come to take her home? Didn't he know she was lost in the prairie? He had warned her about the danger of wandering off in the tall grass and getting lost.

Megan let the tears come. She wailed and cried, and Waiting Woman hurried to pick her up and cradle her and sing some silly song she didn't understand.

That night Megan cried herself to sleep where she lay beside Waiting Woman. Nothing the soft spoken Brulé woman said or did for this wonder child helped. At last Megan went to sleep and dreamed of happy times when she was with her other family, the one where she understood what people said.

Then she saw her daddy, standing in the door of their ranch house.

"Daddy, when are you going to bring me home?" Megan called.

But he didn't seem to hear her. Then he vanished, as if he hadn't really been there. Megan sat up scattering the buffalo robes, and woke up screaming and crying again.

7

Vince Lowe came into the Stafford General Store that morning whistling. He had a grin an axe-handle wide and winked at Oran as he weighed out some soda crackers from a barrel for a woman customer. When she paid and left, Oran hurried up to the saloon owner.

"So what are you so happy about this morning, Vince?"

Vince brought out from behind one leg a knife. It was strange looking, with a curved blade and a bone handle. He flipped the wicked looking weapon, caught it by the handle, and laughed.

"This is our ticket to getting rich. I found it jammed into the back door of the saloon this morning. It pinned a small square of fox fur to the door."

"So?"

"So, dummy, it's my return message from Sly Fox, the Southern Brulé we're playing games with. He's ready. He'll meet us tonight at the usual place. We'll bring two rifles as samples and he'll bring some horses just in case. We're in business, partner!"

A customer came in right then and Oran hurried to wait on him. When his purchases were paid for and he left, Oran looked at the knife again. His grin began to broaden as he thought about the two thousand dollars he would clear on this deal. That was more money than the store would make in four years!

"You sure about this damn Injun?"

"As sure as I am of you."

"Where do we meet?"

"In a safe place, due north of town at the Saline River."

"Christ! That's fifteen miles from here."

"Eighteen. Won't you ride eighteen miles to clear three hundred and eighty five dollars, cold cash?"

"Yeah, sure, but. . . ."

"He'll bring at least ten horses, and we take two rifles. We'll take the horses to Vuylsteke's ranch. He owes me money and won't say a word. From there he sells them to other ranchers telling them he needs to raise money."

"When do we meet this Sly Fox?"

"Usual time, at sunset. So we ride out of town about three, then we won't be late.

The rifles will be in boots on our saddles so they won't look out of place."

"Rounds?"

"A hundred rounds for each weapon in our saddle bags. Sweet deal!"

At slightly before 7 P.M. the two merchants from Hays sat on the bank of the Saline River due north of Hays near a lightning gnarled cottonwood tree. The sun had just dropped below the horizon and shadows were deepening into darkness.

Oran heard a movement behind him but before he could react, a sharp knife blade rested against his throat.

"One slice and you are dead, white eye," a strange voice said.

Vince chuckled. "Christ, Sly Fox, I still don't see how you do it. I knew you were coming, I watched for you and suddenly you're on top of us."

The knife slid away from Oran's throat and he turned to see an Indian standing beside him. He wore only a breechclout, a rifle across his back and summer moccasins. He had long black hair and in the shadows his face seemed sharp, chiseled.

Sly Fox pulled the rifle off his shoulder and patted it. "I like the rifles you brought. Not new, but in good working order."

"You took that off our horses and we never

heard . . ." Oran began. "You're a magician."

Sly Fox sat down next to the men and shook his head. "Not magician, I am Indian, Southern Brulé Sioux. All my life I have learned to live with nature, to cooperate with her. Moving through trees and brush is as easy to me as it is for you to go down a boardwalk."

He checked the rifle again. "I can give you two horses for each rifle."

Vince laughed. "Sly Fox, you old horse-trader. You know damn well that weapon is worth seven horses, the best you have."

Sly Fox did not laugh. He simply shook his head. "The weapon is not new, it could break any time. We have no way to repair broken rifles. I can give you three horses."

Vince shook his head. "Not a chance, Sly Fox. You know what it will cost me if I get caught by the law? I'll go to federal prison for twenty years! I'm entitled to a little profit for taking the risk of bringing you fine rifles. I might come as low as six horses per weapon."

Twenty minutes later Sly Fox and Vince shook hands, settling on four and a half horses for each rifle. Nine horses for each two weapons.

"You brought horses with you, I'd guess," Vince said.

"Come, check them," Sly Fox said. The

horses were a hundred yards away. All had their muzzles tied shut with rawhide to prevent them from making small horse talk as soon as they smelled the new horses arriving.

The muzzles came off and Vince inspected the animals. They were sturdy, two looked like former army mounts. Two were little more than Indian ponies. He rejected the last two smaller ones he called colts, but still picked out nine animals.

The trade was made including the two hundred rounds of ammunition.

"I want ten more rifles for 45 horses. Here a week from tonight," Sly Fox said. Again he and Vince shook hands and Sly Fox rode into the night. They heard other Indians herding the ten remaining horses away to the north.

Vince put rope halters on each of the horses, then tied five on one lead line and four on another and they began moving back toward Hays and the ranch owned by Yancy Vuylsteke.

Oran had a question that had been plaguing him.

"Vince, that redskin talked English good as you and me. How come?"

"Told you already. This was the kid who got lost in a snowstorm, was found by a rancher, and taken in and nursed back to health. They taught him English and he stayed three years before he went back with his tribe. Now he's some sub chief or has his own band or something. Best damn contact I ever had inside the tribes."

"You did good bargaining with that savage," Oran said. "Damn, I would have caved in at three horses. You know, we still gonna make damn near three hundred and fifty dollars, just tonight!"

"Learned that from my old daddy. He bought and sold horses, traded now and then. He could start out in the morning with a mule and have himself a thousand dollar race horse before the day was over."

It took them half the night to trail the nine horses into the Vuylsteke ranch, eight miles northeast of Hays, roust out the rancher and get him to put special ear tags on the horses so they could be sure which ones they had brought in. He was instructed to sell them as soon as he could but not for less than $40 a head.

Back in town the partners sat in the Outlaw Saloon. It was still only eleven o'clock. The bar was booming and the gaming tables full.

A half hour later both men were a little drunk. Their talk about the night's work had begun in whispers, but after mixing beer and whiskey they became less cautious.

"Ten goddamned horses!" Oran yelped.

Both men laughed.

"No, Oran, nine goddamned horses!" Vince corrected him.

They both roared again with glee.

A civilian named Nance Adderly, who sometimes scouted for the army, stood at the bar near where the two men drunkenly congratulated each other. He grinned at their antics. But the idea that the men were talking about selling or buying horses, interested Adderly. He had a small horse farm north of town where he was trying to raise enough good quarter horses to take care of the local demand as well as customers east into the Kansas heartland. He wasn't above finding out the name of a rancher buying horses. He listened closer while pretending to get drunk.

Oran put his arm around Vince's shoulder and whispered in his ear. The whisper could be heard halfway across the saloon. Most of the men paid no attention to the two drunks.

"How we know for sure the sombitch will show up in a week with the . . . the fucking horses?"

Vince stared at him, then giggled. He

shook his head and pushed Oran away.

"Dumb store clerk! Said he'd be there. Be there." They both drank again and stared at each other.

"What's the guy's name again?" Oran asked in another whisper that the civilian scout could hear plainly.

"Bill Sly . . . no, not quite . . . Bill Fox . . . no, not right either. I know it. Just a minute, I know it. Sly Fox. Yeah, that's the guy. Sly Fox."

Nance Adderly almost choked on a swallow of beer. He put the mug down and wiped his mouth and nose looking away from the pair in the booth. *Sly Fox?* Half the people in the territory knew about him. Rescued as a child, taught English and civilized, then running back to his tribe of Brulés when he was fifteen.

Why would this pair buy horses from Sly Fox? More importantly, what would they offer in payment? Sly Fox would not want gold or greenbacks. A slow nagging idea kept building in him. One thing every Indian wanted these days . . . rifles. He slid away from the bar and headed for the door.

He needed a good night's sleep so he'd have a clear head bright and early in the morning when he talked to Colonel Adamson out at Fort Hays.

★ ★ ★

Colt Harding was in the office the next morning when Nance Adderly came in and asked to see the Colonel. The First Sergeant scowled. They'd had trouble with this civilian before. He was a scout, but also a drunk.

"What do you want to see him about, Adderly?" First Sergeant Yarnes asked.

"Rather just tell the Colonel, Sergeant."

"Without telling me, you won't get a chance to tell him, Adderly. Give."

"I think some locals are selling rifles to Sly Fox."

"Oh, damn!" Sergeant Yarnes scowled. "You better come with me." He took the scout to the colonel's door, knocked and then went in. Colt was right behind him.

Colonel Adamson was working over a new dispatch case from Ft. Leavenworth.

"Sir, Adderly here might have something important," Sergeant Yarnes said, then glanced at Colt and left the room.

Adderly told them the story quickly.

"Just drunk talk between friends?" Colonel Adamson asked.

"Don't think so, sir. Stafford runs the general store. He could order a dozen or two rifles and nobody would think a thing about it. Sly Fox speaks English good as I do. Sounds damned suspicious. Thought I

151

should tell you. And . . . sir, if you do go after Sly Fox and need a scout, I know that area."

Colonel Adamson nodded and wrote something on a piece of paper.

"Indeed we will, Mr. Adderly. Give this to the First Sergeant. It's authorization for five days Scout pay at two dollars a day. We appreciate your help in town."

"Yes sir, Colonel sir!" Adderly nearly shouted. He grabbed the paper and hurried out the door.

The colonel looked at Colt. "What do you think?"

"Is Adderly reliable?"

"Almost worthless as a scout in the field, but in town he has a good ear. It's hard to know what's going on in there. The civilians are a tight knit little group. On balance, I'd say he believes he heard what he told us."

"Ten horses. What's a rifle worth these days in horses to an Indian?" Colt asked.

"As always, it depends on what they can bargain for. I've heard about some deals going a horse for a rifle. Again some Indians will go three or four horses per rifle."

"They're getting cheated. A rifle isn't worth more than six, eight dollars at the most."

"They deal in horses, not dollars," Colonel Adamson said.

"Glad it's your baby, Colonel. I've got to do some training on that Lightning Troop. They've had a full day to rest up."

Colt had called for a special drill at ten that morning. He took the Lightning Troop a half mile into the prairie and with the help of Short Grass and three Pawnees began instructing the men in how to ride off the saddle and shoot under the neck of the mount.

Three men out of five fell the first time they tried it. All received only scrapes and bruises and a round of teasing from the men who hadn't tried it yet.

Slowly the men caught on to the trick of holding on by one stirrup and the saddlehorn. The saddle had to be cinched up tight or it would simply slip around to the horse's belly when the side pressure of a 160 pound or heavier man was applied. Two men went down after that fashion.

At high noon Colt took the troop another mile south to a light fringe of woods along a stream.

"Here you have five minutes to gather dry wood, and to build a smokeless fire for cooking. Dismount and tether your horses and stand by."

The men had watched the Indians do the same thing, but now it was a different matter. Colt watched them and when all were dismounted he fired one of his pistols in the air.

"Go" he shouted and checked his pocket watch.

Those men who had watched the Pawneee had a good little smokeless fire burning well before the deadline. Half the men gave up and used any wood they could find and a resulting pall of smoke soon hung over the brush line.

"Sergeants, take the names of those who pass and who didn't. Those who didn't pass will be the fire makers and cooks for the next outing."

Lieutenant Danalaw and the three sergeants all made fires, too. All passed the test.

They had no rations. No one had any noon time dinner.

In the afternoon they worked at picking up a downed rider and riding double.

"In a cavalry engagement with mounted hostiles, a man who has lost his mount has an eighty percent chance of losing his life. This little maneuver is simple, yet can save your life."

That morning Colt had found one man from First Squad who knew how to pick up a rider off the ground. He and Colt practiced twice and were ready that afternoon to give a demonstration.

Colt had Private Garrison ride out twenty yards and dismount and walk away from his horse. Colt rode toward the man at an easy gallop, slowed a little, and just before Colt got to the man, Garrison turned and ran with the horse, grabbed the saddle horn and Colt's hand and swung up behind him on the horse in one easy move.

The troops cheered.

Colt changed places with Private Garrison and hoisted himself onto the back of the mount behind the saddle.

The troops cheered again.

After that it was a slow, one-on-one, training session as Colt, Private Garrison and two of the Indian scouts demonstrated and instructed the men in the pickup.

Man after man tried it, first at a canter, then at a gallop. Those who passed went to one side, the others tried it again. Before they rode wearily into the fort parade grounds at four that afternoon, three-quarters of the troop had passed the pickup test.

Three other troops of cavalry had lined up on the parade ground that afternoon. Colt rode to them and requested a chance to give a demonstration.

He sent four of his men out for the pickup maneuver, then had two men ride past, slip off the horse to the side and pretend to fire a pistol under the horse's neck.

The maneuver brought cheers from the other cavalry. When he had control again, Colt came in front of the men and called out his invitation.

"The Lightning Company is looking for a few good riders who want to be in the best trained unit in the U.S. Army. Anyone who wants to work hard, get expert training, and at least twenty rounds a week target practice is asked to sign up for a transfer to this unit at the Lightning Troop head-quarters immediately following evening mess."

He rode back to his unit and had them dismissed by Lieutenant Danalaw, who caught up with him as he rode to the fort commander's office.

"Sir, this is a surprise to me. Do you think we'll get any takers?"

Colt grinned. "Twenty at least. We'll take the best of the lot. Tomorrow we start physical training."

"What?"

"Exercises, running, lifting, and also target practice."

"We have to buy the rounds? Colonel Adamson says we don't have any rounds to waste."

"No, we don't have to buy our own rounds. I've ordered twenty thousand rounds with General Sheridan's authorization. It doesn't do any good to shoot a rifle if the trooper pulling the trigger can't hit anything.

"We start with target practice in the morning, then physical training in the afternoon. Every man must pass the marksmanship test, must *qualify on his rifle,* to stay in the Lightning Troop."

After mess call that evening they had thirty troopers sign up for the Lightning Troop. They were told to report to their First Sergeant, notify him to put them on TDY to Lightning Troop for two weeks. By then they would either be in the troop or sent back to their old units.

That evening Colt had a call from the Fort Commander. He'd like to talk a minute. Colt followed the messenger back to Colonel Adamson's office and slid into the chair next to his big desk.

"This talk about selling the Indians guns. I've decided to take it seriously. One of my men found Nance Adderly. He's sobering him up, and planting him in the Outlaw Saloon with just enough money to drink but still stay sober.

"A week from today, we'll have a man in civilian clothes watching the saloon, and another one watching the general store. If either man leaves, we'll know it. I also want to have a small patrol of ten men stationed two miles north of town in that woodsy patch next to the trail.

"If Lowe and Stafford are moving north to meet Indians, we'll relieve them of their rifles, and move north with them."

"I'd like to be involved," Colt said. "Short stopping two dozen rifles heading to the Indians now, could save a lot of cavalry blood later on."

"You can lead the patrol. If they start out, we'll try to get a man up to you without being seen."

"Done. If they decide to move earlier, can that scout find out and let us know?"

"That's his job. I just hope he can stay sober long enough to do it."

Juliana Bainbridge had worn one of her prettiest dresses. It exposed a generous round of each breast and the cleavage between them formed a deep shadow. She sat on the sofa next to Lieutenant R. J. Turnball and studied the cards he had played out on a low table in front of them.

"I don't understand. Why can a deuce of spades take an ace of hearts?"

"Because it's trump. I explained that. One suit becomes all powerful once it's named trump."

"Oh, R.J., this is so tiresome. I have a better idea." She leaned toward him, put her hand on the back of his neck and pulled him forward and kissed him. He nearly froze with delight and fear and apprehension. She held the kiss a moment, then eased away.

"Did you like that, R.J.?"

The young lieutenant tried to move his legs to accommodate a growing erection. He mumbled something and Juliana leaned forward again and this time he met her. The kiss was longer, warmer. When she moved back this time she saw that his eyes were closed. She smiled.

"Now, R.J., isn't that just ever so much more fun than playing with dumb old cards?"

"Oh, yes, but. . . ."

"I told you, mother is gone for the afternoon. That's why I suggested you come over." She smiled and traced her finger around his jaw. "Such a handsome face, so strong and military." She kissed him again and he moaned softly.

Juliana smiled at him. "R.J. sweetheart, would you like to . . . you know, touch me?"

He frowned at her, not sure what she meant. She took his hand and placed it on her bare breast top.

He gasped, looked at her, and when she smiled this time he bent to kiss her. The kiss was long and hot and his hand explored her pure white breasts.

Just then Major Bainbridge hurried into the living room. He looked at his daughter being kissed and fondled. The pair came apart instantly.

"Oh, lord!" R.J. whispered. He stood at once. "Sir! I apologize. It was entirely innocent, I assure you!"

"You're excused, Lieutenant. I'll see you in my office in ten minutes."

R.J. picked up his hat and the riding crop he had taken to carrying, and hurried out the door without another glance at Juliana.

Once he was out the door, Juliana giggled. "He was absolutely stunned when you walked in so fast, Daddy."

"I was a little surprised at what I saw. I've told you exposing that much breast is going to get you in trouble."

"Oh, pooh, daddy. Every girl does it. The fancier the ball, the more expensive the dress, the more of a lady's breast can show.

That's the rule."

"I suppose at a ball for a Four Star General, all the women would come bare to the waist."

"Oh, daddy, be reasonable. Please don't punish R.J. I guess I led him on a little."

"You really shouldn't tease these impressionable young men. I don't want any duels fought over you."

"Oh pooh, daddy. Nobody is that silly. I just like both of them. One of them will win out soon, then I'll be safely married to an officer and you won't have to worry about me being an old maid."

"That was one of my least worries. I left an envelope of papers here last night, I just had to come get them. You remember I won't always be here to rescue you from amorous suitors."

"Oh, pooh, daddy. I can handle any man I've ever met. They are like little boys."

"You behave yourself, young lady. I can ship you back to Chicago to your Aunt Louise who will keep an iron hand on you, if I say so. She said something about having a chastity belt all ready for you until you're safely married."

Juliana giggled. "You wouldn't dare say that if mama was here."

"Of course not. Now you mark my word."

He found the envelope and hurried out the door.

Juliana went to the cutler's store to buy some hard candy, and there she found her two closest girl friends. One was Marcy, a year younger, and Lidia, a year older. She reluctantly told them about R. J. Turnball being caught kissing her by her father. The girls promised on their grandmother's honor they wouldn't tell a soul.

Juliana walked home humming to herself. Before retreat that evening at five o'clock, half the people on the post would know about her kissing Lieutenant Turnball. Juliana laughed right out loud. It was exactly what she hoped would happen.

Just after six that evening she was going to the cutler's store for some salt, when Lieutenant Ben Danalaw caught up with her. He was angry, she knew that at once. She was surprised at how angry. He caught her and pushed her against the side of a building.

"Is it true?" he asked.

"What if it is? He's a nice man."

"But . . . but you kissed me. I . . . you said you'd come on the picnic with me. I thought that you and I . . . I mean, we have sort of an understanding. . . ." He broke off when he saw no encouragement.

"Lieutenant Ben Danalaw, kissing a man

does not mean I am engaged to him. I don't belong to you, or any other man. I can entertain whomever I like."

She saw him wilt.

"Of course, now if either one of you does something truly heroic, outstanding . . . then I'd be totally impressed."

"I have to prove myself?"

"Oh, no, goodness sakes. You've done that. You're an officer, a veteran of the Civil War. Goodness no. I like you, Ben, but . . . well, I like R.J. too."

"We'll see about that. We'll damn well see!"

Ben charged off with fire in his eyes. Juliana was sure that she had nudged him into being a little more serious about her. If not, she'd think of something else.

8

A rider with his mount lathered up came storming up to the Fort Hays Commander's office at 9:30 the next morning. He jumped off and rushed inside.

"First Sergeant, Lieutenant Jacobs wishes to report two deserters. They slipped away from the wood cutting detail just after we arrived. They've been gone for two hours. Headed east."

The First Sergeant hurried in to tell Colonel Adamson.

"Damn! Two more. About time we make an example of these deserters. I'd love to catch both and shoot them, but General Sherman won't let us do that.

"Harding, why don't you take fifteen men from your Lightning bunch and try to catch them?"

"What's the usual routine here? They try to jump a passing train?"

"Usually, or just walk on when it stops in Hays. Most of them get away."

Colt Harding scowled. He stood and turned around. "I hate to hunt our own men . . . but I guess we should."

He left quickly and ten minutes later two squads of Lightning Troops rode through the front gate. Lieutenant Danalaw had been assigned as Officer of the Day at the fort and couldn't go with his men.

Colt talked with Sergeant Ivanar, Lightning's Top Sergeant.

"I understand they usually try for the railroad."

"Yes sir. No need to go out to the wood lot. We can angle over to the rails and try to pick up the pair of tracks. Shouldn't be hard."

"Sergeant, this isn't my favorite assignment either, but we're following orders. We try to find them and bring them back if we can."

"I know sir. First time I've ever hunted some of our own men. It don't sit none too good, sir."

They picked up the tracks a mile or so down. The two riders were moving fast. Colt sent his best trackers galloping ahead a quarter mile at a time to check to be sure they were still following the right pair. As the hoof prints were confirmed, a new rider would gallop out ahead of the main party to again search out the tracks a quarter of a mile ahead. This way the Lightning Troop could move as quickly as the deserters.

"When is the next train past here heading east?" Colt asked.

Sergeant Ivanar shook his head. "No idea, sir. I hear the whistles, but don't pay that much attention. As I recall there's one train each way, every day."

By midday they were twelve miles down the train tracks. They had passed one small ranch, but the hoof prints continued straight ahead.

By one o'clock the tracker called to Colonel Harding.

"Sir, you better look at this."

Colt dismounted and walked up to where the private knelt in some soft ground on the right of way.

"See how these prints are irregular? Then one hoof is dragging dirt forward. It makes an uneven pattern. One of them horses up front is going lame."

"I agree. Sergeant Ivanar, send the next tracker out two miles, maybe he can see the deserters."

They rode.

A mile farther along they met the scout. He pointed away from the tracks.

"Sir, they turned off. There's a small

ranch about a mile south. Thought I heard some rifle fire, but it's all quiet now."

Colt took the troop south at a gallop for half a mile, then they slowed to a canter. When they came over a small rise in the prairie, they saw what was left of a small ranch. The frame house had burned to the ground with only wisps of smoke lifting away from it.

They galloped again. Colt saw a body in the yard. The barn and small corral had not been burned but he saw no horses, no stock. As they charged into the farm yard the whole scene was as quiet as a graveyard.

The body by the well was a man. Farther along behind where the house had been they saw a man's torso in a blue army shirt.

Colt rode over and examined the man. An army rifle lay beside him. His legs had been burned to the bone by the house fire. His pants had burned off and half of his shirt.

Sergeant Ivanar shouted from near the barn. Colt rode over and saw the second deserter. His army uniform was intact, but he had three arrows in him and his scalp was gone. They found a woman fifty yards in back of the house as if she had been running for the safety of a line of brush near a small creek. She, like the rest, had been scalped.

The men checked the whole area, but could find no children, living or dead.

"Place isn't big enough to have any ranch hands," Colt said as he assembled the troops. A soldier had come from the barn with a shipping tag on a new one-row walking plow. It was a twelve inch blade and weighed 93 pounds and had cost $8.54, the tag showed. The blade had never seen a furrow.

Colt read the name. "J. B. Willis, Hays, Kansas."

It took them two hours to bury the Willis family. They did the same for the two troopers. Colt took personal effects, such as they were. The army mounts were gone and all the weapons except the one army rifle. Colt decided when the hostiles left the fire had been too hot for them to get close enough to take the rifle.

Colt put it in his report when they got back to the base. Both men evidently had gone up to the ranch to get some food or to trade horses for a sound one. The savages must have hit the place while they were there and the soldiers had helped defend the ranch.

"Recommend that both men be listed as being killed in action against the hostiles, and such facts permanently entered in their records," Colt wrote in his report.

Colt folded the paper and handed it to Colonel Adamson. He agreed with the conclusion.

"I'll write up my run down and get it off through channels first thing."

"How's the other matter coming along, the possible sale of rifles to Indians?"

"Not a glimmer. Haven't heard anything from my spy in the Outlaw Saloon. Two more days until the week will be up. I think I'll turn that one over to you. Use a blocking patrol or handle it anyway you want to."

"Thanks for a hard job."

Colt looked at the map of the area on the wall. New tabs of paper on the Solomon and Bow showed where the nearly 600 Indians were camped. Each note had the date when they were observed.

"You want another run up to the Beaver, Sappa and the Prairie Dog Rivers to check on hostiles?"

"Not unless Sheridan demands it. That's getting well up in the edge of the area we're responsible for."

"Good, I'm not over the last ride yet. You suppose that old scout was trying to fool us on that gun running story?"

"Doubt it. Nance Adderly is honest as the day is long, when he's sober. He's got a little horse ranch out a ways. Trouble is, he has a hard time staying sober."

"Think I'll go into town and have a chat with him — as a civilian. Almost nobody knows me in town."

A half hour later, Colt had changed into some civilian clothes he always carried with him, put on a slouch hat that covered up half of his face, and stepped into the Outlaw Saloon.

He found Adderly at a corner table nursing a beer. Colt got a beer from the bar and went over and sat down across from him.

"Looking for some good cattle working horses, you have any?" Colt asked.

Adderly looked up, his eyes clear. He frowned for a moment then grinned. "Might. Meet me outside by the hardware store. Couple of lean-back chairs down there."

Colt moved on with his beer. He watched a poker game in session, put down the half-finished beer on a table and wandered out.

A few minutes later, Adderly pushed back the chair in front of the Hardware and leaned against the wall. Colt sat the next chair.

"Lost your uniform, Colonel?"

"Nope. You hear anything more about horses?"

"Yep. Yancy Vuylsteke has ten head for sale out at his spread. He never has more horses than he needs. Blamed if I know where they come from. Oh, Yancy owes the hustler who owns the Outlaw Saloon over three thousand dollars on a gambling debt."

"Peculiar?"

"Mighty. He could be selling the horses that come from Injun land few days ago."

"Any more talk about another sale coming up?"

"Nope. Oran is in to the saloon after his store closes every night. Last night Vince left with him for half an hour. They headed toward the general store, but can't say for sure they went there."

"Good. Sounds like a meet is still in the offing. You stay sober and take care."

Colt tipped his chair down and without glancing at Adderly, walked back down the street toward his mount. He looked in some store windows, then mounted up and rode out of town to the north. It took him a half hour to circle the town and head back south to Fort Hays.

Two days later, Colt had Lieutenant Danalaw and twelve men from Lightning

Troop in a patch of heavy brush a mile north of Hays. They were on the trail before it branched out in three directions.

The troop had ridden due west, then cut back once they were out of sight of the town. Now, just after midday, they dismounted and settled down for a wait. Colt had no idea when the gun runners might ride, if indeed they did. North was the most worthwhile gamble.

At three-thirty that afternoon one lookout in the tallest tree that would hold his weight, reported what he guessed were three riders heading north from town.

"Come down," Colt called to the lookout.

Lieutenant Danalaw roused his men and placed them in a line of skirmishers facing the trail which passed fifty yards away. They were completely hidden.

"Colonel, if it's the gun runners, what are my orders?" Lieutenant Danalaw asked.

"Two choices. We take them down here, or we follow them to the exchange."

"We take them here all we have are men and rifles. No criminal activity."

"Precisely, Danalaw. We follow them to the exchange. When they make the switch, we hit them hard, the savages as well, and we keep the guns from moving."

They lay in the heavy brush and watched

as the riders came in sight. Two men on horseback, one led a pack mule with canvas wrapped bundles on each side in a sling.

"Could be rifles," Colt whispered to Danalaw. "That one man I know, the general store owner, Oran Stafford."

"We've got them!" Lieutenant Danalaw said softly.

Colt let the gun runners get nearly a mile ahead, then they moved out, half the troop on each side of the pair. They used a connecting file to keep them in sight.

Nearly two and a half hours passed before the pair stopped. They came to rest on the near side of the Saline River under a lightning scarred cottonwood.

Colt moved his troops in from both sides. There was enough brush along the Sabine so his men could get within a hundred yards of the gun runners without being seen. Colt settled his six men down and made sure all had good fields of fire at the meeting spot.

On the other side, Lieutenant Danalaw did the same thing.

Then everyone waited.

It was six-thirty and the sun was hanging low in the western sky, when Colt saw the first indications of visitors. A lone Indian warrior lifted up on the far side of the Saline and stared at the two white merchants. He raised his hand and four more red men came out of the brush and waded across the river.

The conversation was a mumble, too low to be overheard. Stafford unwrapped the bundles from the pack mule and lifted out a rifle.

The troopers had been ordered not to fire until Colt gave the command. They tensed and waited. The five red men inspected each of the ten rifles, then the tallest one nodded. He signalled and a herd of horses came across the shallow Saline, prodded by six mounted Indians.

When the warriors moved to pick up the rifles, Colt bellowed at them. "Hold it! Don't move. We've got thirty U.S. Army rifles trained on you. Move and you're dead."

The Indians dove at once for the ground. Stafford and Vince Lowe drew their pistols and fired at the direction of the voice.

"Open fire!" Colt shouted.

The volley of gunfire cut down both white men at once, and downed three of the Indians. Two made it to the river and thrashed across.

The herd of horses scattered as the mounted Indians whirled and raced for the river.

Lieutenant Danalaw burst from his hiding place with six mounted men and gave chase after the hostiles.

Colt ordered his men to cease fire when the mounted troopers came within their field of fire.

Colt lifted from where he lay and charged ahead with the other troopers. One fallen Indian near the rifles tried to fire a rifle, but the wounded warrior was killed by three slugs from weapons held by nervous trooper trigger-fingers.

Oran and Vince were both dead.

Colt heard firing, ordered his horse up from the man holding it, and spurred after the running gunfight he heard ahead.

He came to an open spot across the river and found one trooper down, his horse grazing. A dead Indian sprawled a few yards farther on. A second trooper held his shoulder but kept his saddle.

Lieutenant Danalaw charged into a wooded section across a two hundred yard wide open space.

Colt winced, hoping the officer would be lucky. He had only one man with him and there was no telling how many savages might be hidden in the woods.

He heard rifle fire, then a pistol barked and Colt smashed through light brush to the center of the woods. Two Indians saw him coming and spurred away. Colt saw Lieutenant Danalaw's horse standing to the side. He rode over and looked down at the young officer. He had taken two arrows and two rifle rounds to his chest.

Two more troopers raced into the woods, and stopped quickly when they saw the death scene.

Colt slid off his mount and checked Danalaw. He was dead. For a moment Colt swore softly, then motioned to the troopers to lift the Lieutenant onto his saddle and tie him on. His hands and feet were lashed together under the mount's belly.

They moved slowly back to the exchange site. The trooper killed in the meadow was tied on his horse, and then they rode across the Saline.

Sergeant Ivanar had secured the weapons on the mule and had a lead line tied. Colt decided to bring the two civilians back to Hays. It might be a good object lesson for anyone else with a hankering to get rich quick by selling rifles to the hostiles.

They spent a half hour rounding up what of the horses they could. At last they bunched thirty-five animals and six of the best cowboys in the troop began herding the horses back toward the fort. They would put them in the remount corral. At least half of them would eventually be broken, trained and become army mounts.

Colt figured he had just saved the army over a thousand dollars in horseflesh.

They rode into town just after nine o'clock. The two civilian bodies were laid out in front of the town marshal's office. Quickly a crowd gathered and stared at the men in the glow of coal oil lanterns.

The men were recognized at once. The ten rifles had been laid between the men. Colt explained the situation to Marshal Menville.

"Got what was coming to them," the marshal said. He said he'd take the bodies to the undertaker. "First, I'm gonna let them stay there until midnight so anybody who wants to can come take a look."

Colt continued the mile south to Fort Hays and reported to Colonel Adamson who was still in his office. Word jolted through the troops like a runaway freight train.

Before Colt had half the story told to Colonel Adamson, his door burst open and Major Bainbridge and his daughter stood there. The girl was crying.

"Is it true about Lieutenant Danalaw?" the major asked.

"Yes, he's dead," Colt said.

Juliana's face turned into a hate-mask. She screamed and ran at Colt, hitting him with her fists until her father caught her and held her.

"You killed him! You killed Ben. You never have liked him. Colonel, you killed the man I loved!"

Major Bainbridge said something they couldn't hear through Juliana's ravings. He walked her out of the room, still holding her tightly from behind. Colt took a deep breath, closed the office door and looked up at Colonel Adamson.

"Colonel, I don't know what possessed the young man. I've seen him under enemy fire. He was always calm, organized, did what he knew was the best thing to do.

"Here he pursued the hostiles without specific orders. He charged across the river and then into thick brush when he had only one man left. He must have known there could be an ambush waiting for him inside that wooded section. It was a showoff move, sir. Like he was trying to prove something. I'll never understand it."

"Strange what some men will do in the heat of battle. You've seen it dozens of times." He looked at the map. "Damn! At least you stopped the gun runners and brought back some horses. Oh, don't put any of the speculation into your report about the death charge. No sense putting any cloud over the young man."

"I'll keep it honorary, sir," Colt said.

When he was through, Danalaw might even get a posthumous medal. Colt would make the incident read like a dime novel.

He stopped by the Bainbridge quarters and talked to the Major.

"Harding, I was completely surprised. Juliana has been courted by these two officers. I didn't think she had really made up her mind yet. When she heard the news she threw a screaming, wild-eyed fit. That's the only way I can describe it. Took me a half hour to get her calmed down enough to go see Colonel Adamson. You saw what happened next."

"How is she?"

"Doc Constatine gave her a powder. He said it would calm her down and help her sleep. Before she dropped off she begged me to send her back to Chicago. She said in Chicago people don't get killed all of the time. If she still wants to go after a week or so, we'll put her on the train."

Colt told the Major again that he was sorry, and went over to his own quarters. He took out a picture of his family. He had had it made into a tintype so he could carry it with him. Doris his wife, and little Sadie his five year old, and Daniel who was almost four.

As he looked at Sadie, he thought again about the Freening girl, the one they never found. She was officially listed as missing, but Colt knew that she had been captured. He would listen for any word of a white child in any Brulé camp. The town people said the little girl's name was Megan and she had long blonde hair and blue eyes.

The similarity of it hit him a sudden blow. Tomorrow he would see what he could find out about little Megan.

The next morning Colt found a message for him at the Commander's office. He opened it and read it with interest.

"Colonel Harding. I understand you have some close ties with General Sheridan, the Indian butcher. I have an urgent need to talk with you. If you could arrange your priorities and your busy schedule, I would appreciate your coming to my brother's house at 145 First Street at ten A.M. today. Thank you very much. Mrs. Millicent Kane. Please R.S.V.P. My messenger will await your reply."

Colt snorted and showed the note to Colonel Adamson.

Adamson pulled at his mutton chops and then stared out the window. "I'm suggesting that you go see what she wants. She's a regular harridan, a damn do-gooder, but not much we can do about her except keep her as soft spoken as possible. See what she wants."

Colt bit off his quick response. Colonel Adamson laughed and shook his head. "If it wasn't you, she'd be after me. I'm just taking advantage of Phil Sheridan's posting you here. Maybe you can do some good mending army fences with the woman."

"I could turn you down on this," Colt said with a touch of a bite in his voice.

"Could, but I don't think you will. For one thing, you're curious and she's a right smart looking woman."

They both laughed.

Promptly at ten that morning, Colt stepped down from his army mount and tied him to the post in front of Millicent Kane's address. As he walked up the path to the front steps, the door came open.

"Colonel Harding, I would guess," a woman's voice said. Then Millicent Kane stepped into the morning light.

She was much as Colt had remembered her, at least five-feet eight inches tall, far above average, with long brown hair. She was slender and pretty with wide set green eyes and a small, almost snub nose.

He stepped on the porch and took her hand which she offered just like a man.

"Good morning, Miss Kane. I'm a minute early, I assume that will be all right."

"If the tea is steeped, it will be fine." She flashed a smile, turned and went into the parlor.

The room was neat, well appointed and had a homemade, braided rug on the floor. Its circles of inch wide braids went around and around in increasing width until the entire floor was covered. The big rug spread more than 12 feet in diameter.

"I've never seen a braided rug quite so large," Colt said.

"My sister-in-law. It's her hobby."

Mrs. Kane poured tea and offered him cream, sugar or lemon. He took only the lemon.

"Lemon, that shows character. I should be reading tea leaves."

She straightened her shoulders. "Colonel Harding, I understand your men shot down Mr. Stafford and Mr. Lowe last night. Is that correct?"

"The two men were trading rifles and ammunition to Indians for horses. Such activity, as you know, is against federal law. We were acting in our capacity to uphold federal law in regards to the indigenous Indian population."

"You were authorized to use deadly force?"

"Are you joking, Mrs. Kane? If so, I have much more important things to do."

"Like shooting down five American Indians? You also killed that number last night, as I have discovered."

Colt stood. "Mrs. Kane, thank you for the tea. I'll try to remain civil until I'm out your front door."

"Sir, if you are a gentleman, you will return to your seat and listen to what I have to say. Then, as intelligent adults, I will listen to what you have to say. Agreed?"

Colt sighed. Mending army fences. He took a deep breath, looked longingly out the window and sat down.

"Thank you. Yes, I am fighting for the American Indian. He is the forgotten man in this power mad rush to the West. Do you realize that at one time the American Indian, in their hundreds of tribes, *owned and occupied* this whole land we call the United States? All 3,623,420 square miles of this land including states and territories were roamed over by thousands and thousands of

American Indians, Mexican Indians, and some from the far north.

"We stole it. Colonel Harding, *we stole all of that land from the native American Indians.* Wouldn't you fight if somebody stole your gun, your horse, your house, your ranch . . . your whole *nation?*

"I've heard people who say the only good Indian is a dead Indian. That's shocking. These men and women, these *children* are human beings, just like you and me. Do they not bleed like we do? Do they not laugh and cry and wail and lament and rejoice like we do? They're human beings.

"So why does the army continue to hunt them down like animals and slaughter them like deadly rattlesnakes? Don't you think it's time the army worries about defending our borders from attack by outside forces, and leave the Indians alone?"

She had been pacing back and forth as she spoke, pointing her finger and balling a fist now and then for emphasis. When she finished, she sat down.

Colt stared at her a moment. "Mrs. Kane, did you know the Freening family? If you knew them even slightly, you must have some compassion for them, but I've heard none. Two days ago a man and wife 18 miles east of town were cut down by the Indians, scalped and their house burned to the ground.

"Where is your tenderness for them and your indignation against the murderers who perpetrated these crimes?

"The Indians are just like us? Not a chance, Mrs. Kane. I've lived with Indians, the Oglala Sioux. I've been through one of their tests of manhood. I know how they think. Let me spell it out for you.

"The Indians are a warrior class of people. They live by the warrior code, by the warrior way of life. That means the men are raised and trained from childhood to be warriors, to defend the camp, the band. But more importantly, to learn how to go on raids.

"The Freenings were the end result of an Indian raid. What does an Indian do on a raid? They are just like we are, you said. Of course. The hardware store man goes to work, sells nails and bolts and roofing paper. That's his work. There is nothing moral or immoral about it, right? That's his job.

"The warrior does the same thing. When he goes to work he kills men, women and children from an enemy tribe, or from a white farmer or village. He rapes and plunders the women and their homes, he steals the cattle and the horses and guns and axes

185

and metal to make his war arrows.

"This is the warrior's line of work. Nothing moral or immoral about it. He is not angry at the white settlers. He is not furious at the wagon trains or the railroad workers. It's simply his job to raid. That means taking prisoners and slaves. If the prisoners or slaves don't act properly, he kills them. There is no good or bad involved, no morality, it's his way of life.

"Let me tell you about a warrior and his sport. He had a Mexican slave who bore him a child. The warrior was angry because the child came out looking all Mexican. The warrior took the infant, who was only a month old, tied a rawhide rope to her foot and threw her into blackberry vines with vicious thorns. The child was pulled out of the vines screaming as the thorns tore into her naked flesh. A dozen times the baby was thrown into the thorns and the warrior screeched with laughter every time. When the child was not dead after the tenth time through the thorns, the warrior leaped on his war pony and dragged the bleeding hardly recognizable body through the woods. When he came back after a mile's ride, he cut the bloody mass off his rawhide rope and threw it on a trash heap where it froze that night.

"That is the warrior ethic, Mrs. Kane. Nothing moral or immoral about it. I find a lot of trouble in supporting anyone who chooses this kind of savage society and puts it over our civilized society. If those cold blooded killers, rapists and defilers are your friends, then *I* do not wish to be one of your friends."

Colt stood, nodded his goodbye, and left the house.

When he looked back at the door, Mrs. Kane sat where she had been. She did not move as he walked away, only a vacant, shocked, stunned expression remained on her face.

9

Chief Running Bear sat in his tipi near the Republican River just over the border in the state of Nebraska. He made sure the flap was down on the tipi entrance, then he laughed and played with the small white girl, Little Sunflower.

She had captivated him during the past two weeks. She seemed drawn to him, asking him questions he couldn't understand. He taught her a few words in the Lakotah language, but still it was touch and point and repeat one word over and over.

He lay on his back and held her high over his head, pretended to drop her but caught her. She squealed in delight. Little Sunflower liked to follow him outside, and often he let her go with him. Once he gave her a ride in front of him on his war pony. He had never seen her more pleased.

She still cried herself to sleep some nights, and Running Bear knew she was crying for her lost family. But it was the way of The

People. It was done, finished. Now she was a Brulé Sioux. He would make her the best Brulé woman in the history of the tribe!

Running Bear put her down, gave her a small boat he had made for her and told her to go play with it in the creek with the other girls. She didn't fully understand, but when he pointed at the stream, she laughed and ran that way.

The chief of his own band of a hundred warriors had more pressing business. All but one of the bands he and Swift Bird had contacted would join in the alliance. It would not touch all tribes, but there were enough.

From twelve bands in the immediate area they had over 700 warriors! What a force they would make charging through Fort Hays and then the small town of Hays itself. There would be booty for everyone.

Running Bear was the best war strategist in the group and they had given him command. The men of the tribes would gather at the Big River, which ran into the Smoky Hill to the south of the fort. Most of the bands would move south to the headwaters of the Big River which was two days' ride from the fort.

He planned on riding only at night, so no roaming patrols of Pony Soldiers would spot them. Then at dawn, while the weak garrison soldiers slept, his warriors would sweep down on the fort, set fire to every building, kill or drive out the Pony Soldiers and the foot soldiers and utterly destroy the fort! There would not be a stick of wood or a cooking pot left that the white eye could use to rebuild.

There would not be enough left alive to build anything.

Running Bear smiled. He walked quickly to the council fire and sat down among the others of the twelve.

It had been agreed that each band would bring ten women to cook for them. There would be two travois and the women would all be mounted. That would slow them, but there was no cause for speed. Once the soldiers were killed, their fort burned, they could spend the summer raiding the rest of the white eyes in the whole area.

"We will turn this grassland back to the buffalo. We will let our buffalo brothers roam the hair of Mother Earth and prosper and multiply and serve the needs of The People of the plains forever and forever."

The Council then approved the list of older warriors and young men who would remain behind and guard the camp. Running Bear looked at his fellow warriors.

"There will be much loot to bring home. I can promise each warrior two rifles and two pistols and all of the white eye bullets for the weapons that we can carry. No one will be able to stand up to us when every one of our warriors has four fire arms to defend and attack with. We will rule the plains!"

"What about the Pony Soldiers from other forts?" Walking Dove asked. "There is another nest of the soldiers a long day's ride toward the rising sun along the rails of steel."

"Yes, they will try to find us, to retaliate for their losses. But with our rifles, and on our own territory, we can ambush the smaller units and wipe them out. We will engage the major forces with our superior numbers and kill them to a man. Your scalp pole will be so heavy with Pony Soldier hair that you will be forced to put up two or three scalp poles."

There was a sudden cheer from the council.

It was done.

They would ride the morning of the seventh sun to meet their fellow warriors on the Big River.

The time to attack had come.

Already some bands were on the move. Two whole bands of Brulés had gone south to the headwaters of the Smoky Hill River to be close at hand. Some of the Arapahoes were ready. Two bands of Cheyenne would ride with them. Former angers and hatreds had been swallowed and forgotten. This was a war for their very existence, and The People understood.

Running Bear held the war to be just and necessary. He was sure that with surprise and with seven hundred warriors, they would have no trouble in defeating the Pony Soldiers and infantry at Fort Hays. He would sleep well that night. He left the council fire and walked to the stream.

Little Sunflower was in the middle of the foot deep stream sailing her small boat. Three other small girls splashed in the water playing with her.

Running Bear smiled and walked back to his tipi. There was much to do before they rode south.

Lieutenant Paulson came out of the Fort Commander's inner office and stood talking to the Colonel.

"Sir, what are we supposed to do with these four sets of mirrors and tripods? Somebody said they were helio-something. Can I junk them, or send them back to Leavenworth, or what?"

Colt stood and stepped over to the pair.

"Lieutenant, did you say we have four heliographs here?"

"I guess, if that's what they are. No damn good to me."

Colt grinned. "Colonel, do I have your permission to set up those heliographs? It would take eight men at each of three off-fort positions, and one group here."

"Just what is a heliograph?" Lieutenant Paulson asked.

"Usually a set of two mirrors on a steel frame or a tripod that can be leveled and moved to catch the sun's rays. Then the mirrors are used to send flashes of bright sunshine aimed at a certain spot."

Colonel Adamson broke in. "Yes, yes. I've seen them work. On a clear day you can signal fifteen, twenty miles that way. Depends how big the mirror is, as I recall."

"Right, Colonel. If we could set up three outposts with the helios, we could have instant communication in three directions for fifteen to twenty miles! It would be as good as our own telegraph line."

"You need someone who knows Morse code, right?" Colonel Adamson asked.

"True. We must have a manual on the helio if we have the equipment. We might even find one or two of our men who have been operators before. Even a telegraph operator would be great."

"Go ahead, Harding. Set up your units. First you'll need to get the men trained to use it. By then, you and I will decide where to put the outposts."

That morning Colt dug out the heliographs and checked them. There was an operating manual with Morse code. An announcement at drill produced only one man, Corporal Nelson, who had used a helio before. He was an old hand with six years of duty. He helped Colt set up one unit at one side of the parade grounds, and another unit diagonally across from the first.

Then the mirrors had to be aimed directly at each other. This done, Colt began calling for volunteers for heliograph duty. He soon found six men to learn code as operators. It was slow going, just memorizing the code might take a week.

Colt left Corporal Nelson to finish the training on the men and went to talk with Colonel Adamson.

The commander was ready. "We need intelligence to the east and west and north. Well, not really east and west, more like northeast and northwest. Somewhere about here." He pointed to the map.

"We'll go for a ride and pick out the highest points in these areas," Colt said. "Normally we can see only seven miles out here before the curvature of the earth sends our line of sight out into the sky. The higher we get, the farther we can send our signals."

It took them a full day to pick out the spots. Colt took a foot square hand mirror and flashed the fort from various high points and soon found the best in the three directions.

The next day he took the operators, six infantry guards and one cavalryman as a messenger in case something drastic happened to the team. They marched to the first hill and established a small camp.

Then they leveled off a spot on the hill top, set up the helio and within five minutes contacted the home set on the roof of the two story barracks Number One. Corporal Nelson was there operating.

"Welcome," Corporal Nelson sent.

The helio men on Post One wrote down the dots and dashes and translated the word.

"Send back, thanks," Colt said.

Colt and two extra cavalrymen rode back to the fort. The next day they went out and set up the north post, and the third day Colt established the third on to the northeast.

Colt left the two operators and six men there as guards, and the one man with a horse, and headed back to the fort with his three extra men.

They just left an open stretch and were moving through a small wooded area when Colt heard one of his men groan behind him. The man toppled off his horse and a second man screamed. "Hostiles!" he bellowed.

Colt spurred forward. The hostile's rifle round slammed against his head, smashed him off the mount and toppled him to the ground.

When Colt regained consciousness, he was aware of a smashing, crashing headache. Blood smeared his head and face. He blinked away the blood and saw a fire. It was dark. He saw Indians sitting around the fire cooking meat.

One of his troopers stood against a tree where he had been stripped naked and tied. He showed blood slashes on his chest and arms. The man's head hung but he seemed alive.

Colt was not tied. They must know he was not dead. He couldn't see the horses anywhere. The savages must have stopped for the night, to have some fun torturing the Pony Soldiers. Colt knew his turn was next.

He couldn't identify the tribe.

A warrior went to the captive and used his knife to put a slice down the man's chest. The trooper bellowed in pain and the Indians laughed. Colt saw six of them.

"Stop that at once!" Colt shouted at the gathering in his best rememberd Sioux Lakotah.

The Indians backed off in surprise. Two rushed over to him, knives ready.

"Leave that man alone, he is my friend," Colt roared at them in Sioux. "What are you doing here? This is not your hunting grounds."

The leader of the band came up and put his knife under Colt's chin. Colt stood cautiously and looked down at the shorter man.

"What part of The People are you?"

"We are Oglala Sioux. How do you speak our language?"

"I am blood brother to the great Chief Red Cloud."

"You lie!" the warrior said.

"Give me a blade and the pig of a Oglala will know my blade does not lie."

"How are you blood brother to the great Chief Red Cloud? It is impossible."

"Let me take off my shirt and I'll show you. You know of Red Cloud's test of bravery, his trials of manhood."

"*O-kee-pa,* yes, everyone knows of the torture rite. Only brave Sioux can stand the test."

"I am brave Sioux, blood brother to Chief Red Cloud."

"You lie again!"

"Let me prove it."

Slowly Colt began to take off his shirt. He opened the buttons and pulled it off one arm, then the other, and slowly turned his back to the Oglala so he could see the four scars on his upper back and shoulders.

"Aiiiiiiiiiiyiiiiiiiiiiiiii!" the leader screeched.

The other warriors hurried up with weapons ready, but also cried out when they saw the scars which were left by the torture ritual.

Colt remembered the scene only too well. Two pairs of parallel slices were made in his upper back. A half inch thick green wood sharpened stick was forced through his flesh just under the skin through both slices. A rawhide rope had been tied to the center of the two sticks and he was lifted up and hung by the sticks through his flesh.

To add to his own weight, buffalo skulls were attached to his ankles. He had hung there twenty minutes as the tribal warriors watched. Colt had not fainted and had been let down to continue the ritual.

Now the scars were proof to any Sioux that the agonizing ritual had been experienced and withstood. It made him Sioux brother to them all.

Slowly, Colt put on his shirt.

"You did not believe," Colt said with scorn.

"You are the first white eye ever to pass the test."

"Untie my trooper. Bind up his wounds."

The leader of the group did so himself. Colt checked. He and the wounded man were the only troopers there.

"Two died?" Colt asked.

The Indians nodded.

The leader of the group came up with Colt's army issue pistol and his Spencer. The weapons and clothes of the trooper were brought and he was helped to dress.

"Why are you here, two hundred miles from your camp?"

"We have no camp. We live off the land. This is our land, all of it. We cannot be penned into a tiny pasture like a herd of your white eye buffalo. We must be free to roam Earth Mother and to pick from her fruits."

"There is no place in Kansas where the Sioux may live this way. The Iron Horse, the white men, they come and take your hunting ranges, your buffalo. You must move west if you want the freedom to live as your fathers lived."

"It should not be so."

"What should be and what is so, often are not the same."

The warrior came to Colt and bathed the wound on his head, washed the blood from his face and neck, then applied a potion that he made from a little water and some crushed leaves.

"Your wound will heal quickly. You are free to go when you feel strong enough."

"With the daylight."

"We must go now, reach safer ground."

"Tell my brother, Chief Red Cloud, I wish him well."

The Oglala Sioux nodded.

Colt went to check on his trooper. His name was Warnick and he had been shot in the shoulder with a rifle round. The bullet was in deep.

"Sir, why didn't they kill us?"

Colt told him. The private stared at the officer in amazement.

"You really did that, that torture test?"

"Yes. I was trying to talk Chief Red Cloud into signing the Laramie Treaty. So far, he hasn't. How are you feeling?"

"Hurt like hell, sir."

"I understand. Sleep if you can."

Colt looked up and found the four army mounts had been brought to him as well as the two dead troopers.

The Oglala stared at Colt a moment, nodded and slipped away in the darkness.

Colt tethered the horses, brought blankets from the saddle tie downs and made Warnick comfortable.

"You get some sleep, trooper. We'll ride out of here first thing in the morning, and you'll have tall tales to tell to your grandchildren."

Colt fed the small fire and sat beside its warmth for an hour. Warnick at last dozed off and Colt stretched out on his blanket and thanked Red Cloud again that he had suggested that Colt undergo the ritual of bravery. Today it had saved two lives, one of them his. What a crazy life. What a wild way to make a living.

He snorted. For as long as he lived. If he wasn't careful that might not be long. Only chance saved him this time. He could have been the first one killed in the attack.

Colt felt the booming of the headache come back as soon as he laid down. He moved, sitting up against a small tree with the blanket around him. The headache stopped. Soon he was sleeping.

They created a small sensation the next morning when they rode into the fort about ten o'clock.

Doc Constatine took both of them into his office. He treated the trooper first, pulling out the rifle slug, then binding up his other wounds.

When Doc looked at Colt's head he snorted. "Some damn Injun concoction. Wished I knew what the hell it was. Crushed leaves and water. Anything else? You can't see but it's kept the wound clean and is actually starting it to heal. Damn, wish I knew what plant that was."

"That's enough medical research for today, Doc. Just fix up my head so I can get back to work."

That afternoon, in brilliant Spring sunshine, Colt checked with the three outposts. All were safe and in operation. No hostiles were seen in the area.

Colt warned them about a band of six renegade Oglalas in the area and to watch out for them. Lookouts were maintained dawn to dusk.

A question came in: Can we hunt to eat?

The answer went back quickly to all three: Hunting for game permitted.

Colt slid into his chair next to his small desk. He had pushed the heliographs out to nearly twenty miles. Still, the foot wide mirrors had thrown the sun flash the distance. Now they would have some warning if any large bands of hostiles moved within sight. Not perfect, but better than nothing. He would love to set up telegraph lines to a dozen points 25 miles away in each direction and establish observation and listening posts. But that was out of the question.

Colonel Adamson heard the results of the heliograph and grunted. "Damn things might work."

Colt laughed. "Colonel, this isn't a recent development. Heliographs have been used since the times of the ancient Romans more than 2,000 years ago."

"Good for them," the Commander said and Colt grinned.

10

Later that same afternoon, Colt almost thought of it again. There had been some talk among the Oglalas when they thought he was still unconscious. He remembered hearing it, but not the complete conversation. Something about a gathering . . . he wasn't sure. It would come back to him.

The rest of the day he supervised training the Lightning Company. A new officer had requested the command. Lieutenant Garland had presented himself to Colt, who talked with him for a while and gave him at least temporary command of the Lightning Company. Colt remembered seeing him as an interested party as they did some of their previous training. He was a cavalry officer, a First Lieutenant, with some combat experience.

About three o'clock while the troop worked on firing under the horse's neck, Colt remembered what he had heard the

Oglalas say. He went at once to the Fort Commander.

"Colonel, that's what I heard. I'm not sure it makes sense, or that it's the truth. Those Oglalas were talking about an alliance, a gathering of the tribes in the area to launch an attack on Fort Hays. They were renegades, had left their band and formed a new, small group who would go on raiding deep into the white man's settlements. They had decided not to join in the alliance."

Colonel Adamson paced the small office. He puffed on a half smoked cigar. His hands clasped behind his back.

"Couple of points. Were you rational enough when you were coming out of that head wound to hear straight? Next, if you were, did this renegade band know what was going on? They might not have seen another tribe for two weeks."

"Colonel, I even wake up fast. I'm awake at once and ready for action. Same thing when I came out of that rifle ball along side my skull. I was rational. That's exactly what the Oglalas said. If we can believe them or not — that's the question."

"No Indian tribe I know of has ever attacked a major army installation, even one without palisades. Why would they think of trying it now?"

"Desperation. Put yourself in their shoes. What would you do? The army has been tracking them back to their villages. No one village can take on a large force of Pony Soldiers. But if several bands get together. . . . Seems to make sense to me. Say they got those 600 warriors from tipis we saw on that last patrol, plus another 300 from the Prairie Dog and Beaver Creek areas.

"Would you be willing to attack a fort like this one with 900 men?" Colt asked the Colonel.

"Damn right! They could come at us at night or just at dawn, hit us by surprise, have a damn good chance of winning. All right, I see your point. Let's assume for now that the savages are planning an attack. We'll get ready for one. They live to the north of us, northwest. That's no reason to think they will come at us that way. How would you attack Fort Hays?"

Colt walked to the map. "I'd come from the south and east, the spot least likely to be suspected. Just to keep everyone alerted, I'm going to send a message to our three outposts by helio."

Colonel Adamson looked out the window. "You better hurry, we've got clouds moving in from the west."

Colt went to the roof of Barracks Two

and had Corporal Nelson send the same message to all three outposts:

"Be alert. Possible hostiles moving toward fort. Report any sightings."

By the time the third outpost acknowledged the message, the clouds pushed over the fort and closed down any more communications.

Back in the Commander's office, Colt studied the map. "Too damn much territory," he fumed. "How can we patrol an area two hundred miles square? Ft. McPherson on the Platte River doesn't seem to be doing any work to the south of them."

He traced the Smoky Hill River out toward its end. Ft. Wallace was shown on the map positioned on the stream about 40 miles from the Colorado border.

"What's going on out at Fort Wallace? We hear anything about them from the dispatches?"

"Not a lot. Seems they have a tougher situation out there, with more hostiles and a lot more raids. Their wood gathering people get hit frequently."

"So they aren't a lot of help to us. Christ, I've got to go on another reconnaissance patrol up in there at least to the North Fork of the Solomon again. See what's going on. If I find a lot of nearly empty camps, we'll have some indication."

"Tomorrow?"

"First thing. The Lightning Troop isn't fully trained yet, but it can move faster than any other troop available. I'll go with forty-five troopers and six scouts. Am I authorized?"

"You're shooting your own birds on this one. You've got the orders to do just about as you want. But I agree. We need some information from up there. This is the way to get it."

Lightning Troop left the next morning, rode hard northwest, checked with the heliograph team on what they dubbed round top hill. Then they rode across the Saline and charged north toward the Solomon. They had another twenty-five mile ride and covered the distance in a little less than four hours.

Colt had been pushing them through the most favorable ground, not sticking to the woods and depressions. He didn't care if the hostiles knew they were coming or not.

At the South Fork of the Solomon they turned downstream, eastward and had covered only four or five miles when the scout ahead rode back fast.

The Pawnee, Short Grass, pointed ahead.

"Summer camp. Maybe Brulé. Fifty, sixty tipis."

Colt halted the troop, put them in a wooded area and told them to stay there and be quiet. No gunshots, no loud talk. He rode east with Short Grass to check the sighting.

Colt and the scout crawled up a low ridge and looked down at the camp spread along the river. Something seemed wrong.

Short Grass came up with the trouble first. "No warriors," the Pawnee said. "Old women, children, some old men. No warriors."

"Which means they *are* on a raid, or out to an alliance." Colt took a deep breath and rubbed his face with one hand. "Let's go get the troops."

Lightning Troop attacked the village an hour before sunset. They fired into the tipis from two hundred yards, then charged forward. There were only two shots in response, both from a pistol an old warrior held with both hands. He missed and fell with three rifle bullets in his chest.

Women and children ran from the village. Colt had ordered his men to let them go. For twenty minutes Colt and his troops searched the village. There was no one left.

"Burn it down," Colt commanded.

Troopers with torches ran from one tipi to the next setting them on fire. A dozen mounted troopers found the Indian pony herd a quarter of a mile down stream. The detail had orders to shoot any ponies found. Fifty head were slaughtered with rifle and pistol fire.

By darkness the Brulé camp was destroyed. All pemmican and jerky had been heaped in the flames and burned. Every weapon found was burned. The tall tipi poles, which were hard to locate in Kansas, were fed into the fires until they were consumed. Colt could hear the Brulé women wailing in the woods not far away.

They would learn too, that this was total war, and if they were not on a reservation, they were the enemy.

Colt moved four miles back upstream in the dark and found a place he could defend, a small woodsy area with a bluff at the back. He bedded down the men, let them eat army issue chow and put out double guards.

Lieutenant Garland sipped on a cup of coffee as he looked at Colt across their small cooking fire.

"Sir, this is quite an introduction for me to the Lightning Troop way of warfare. I am pleased, impressed. I'd do everything I can to promote the lightning style of operation.

Lieutenant Danalaw had written down a handbook on the troop. He was always writing something. I have a good outline to go by."

"Good. I'll be around a while to help out. The keys are speed, silence, trained men who can shoot straight, and living off the land. When you hit the hostiles it's total war with the destruction of camps and supplies the number one task."

"Yes sir. Where to tomorrow?"

"We'll look for another camp. One isn't enough to establish a pattern. You've heard about the chance for an alliance by the hostiles in this area. If we find another camp with the warriors gone, we'll know what we came to find out — the hostiles are grouping for an attack on Fort Hays."

In the morning they pushed across the south fork and bypassed the Bow River and headed for the North Fork of the Solomon River. It was a twenty mile ride. When they hit the river they stopped for a break and sent the Pawnee scouts in both directions along the stream.

They came back an hour later. One had found a camp upstream two miles. Colt took the troop for a look. The last quarter mile he and Short Grass moved up on foot through the brush along the river.

They had just passed a young cottonwood

when two Indians screamed and leaped out at them with their knives. Colt had time only to throw up the butt of his Spencer rifle. The heavy stock slammed into the savage's jaw, jolted his head upward sharply and broke his neck.

Short Grass had his knife out and circled the other hostile. Colt had stumbled after killing the man and now came to his knees, his Colt leveled at the savage.

"No shoot!" Short Grass said softly. They were too close to the Indian camp. A shot would bring half the warriors in the settlement to investigate.

Short Grass feinted to the left, jumped in the other direction and tripped the man facing him. Short Grass lunged forward, his knife held like a sword. The Indian hit the ground and rolled, but Short Grass moved with him, the blade slicing into the hostile's chest. The scout ripped the knife sideways and out.

"Cheyenne," Short Grass said as he jumped and looked around. There were no more hostiles.

The Cheyenne warrior looked at Colt, his face clouded with anger, then he rumbled deep in his throat. Blood spilled out of his mouth and his head rolled to one side as he died.

They didn't bother to hide the bodies. In a few minutes it wouldn't matter. When they saw the camp, they found again that most of the warriors were gone.

Colt and Short Grass hurried back to the men. Ten minutes later they attacked the Cheyenne camp from two directions.

"Kill the warriors, drive the women and children into the brush," Colt had instructed the troops. "We're not here to slaughter women and children."

Three warriors ran from tipis as the attack began. All had rifles and fired effectively before they were cut down by the superior force.

The Cheyenne women screamed at the soldiers as they herded them out of the camp. One woman had been killed in the opening barrage. Destruction of the camp took less time than before, the troops were getting efficient at it.

Colt told them to save one parfleche filled with buffalo jerky. They would have something to chew on as they rode.

After two hours of burning and smashing everything of value, the troops headed out of the smoking ruins. As they left, Colt saw the women move back in to see what they could salvage.

There was nothing left.

Colt had seen enough. He turned back south and east, riding hard, heading for the fort. He kept to the best route, the wide open prairie between the rivers. Here in western Kansas the grass was shorter, tougher, as the altitude increased. Near the Colorado border Kansas rose to over 4,000 feet as the land sloped up toward the Rocky Mountains. The general lay of the state was high in the west and north, and lowest in the east and southern parts.

They rode for three more hours, then camped in a brushy section near a stream and watched while the scouts started cooking fires and buried the pheasants and rabbits they had killed for the evening meal.

They reached the fort the next day with no more contact with Indians. Colt went directly to the commander's office.

"So?" Colonel Adamson asked as Colt stalked in.

Colt poured himself a cup of coffee that had been heating on the small stove in the Commander's office, took a long pull, then scowled as he stared at the Colonel.

"I think the alliance is a fact. We hit two villages, one a Brulé, and the other Cheyenne. All but a few of the warriors were out of camp. It's no coincidence. I'm afraid the hostiles are making good on their plans for a grand alliance."

Colt and Colonel Adamson spent the next three hours working out a defensive plan for the fort. If they placed the troopers and infantry around the back of the buildings facing outward, they would have barely enough to circle the whole fort.

"I'd suggest we dig some fortifications in the gaps between the buildings. Trenches where the men can stand and fight."

Colt agreed. They made their plans and slowly moved the fort into a war-time imminent attack status.

Running Bear looked up as a rider streaked into the series of encampments. The rider was a woman. She stopped at a group of warriors. A moment later she turned and rode toward him.

The rider was Waiting Woman, his first wife. There was blood on her shoulder and she sat her pony but slumped forward. He caught her and lifted her to the ground.

"Waiting Woman, you have news?"

"The camp, our camp, destroyed, not a tipi pole left we can use. Our food is all gone, our robes, everything. It was Captain Two Guns!"

Running Bear closed his eyes in anger. He

lifted his hands in supplication, but when his eyes came open they were twin coals of hatred.

"We are gathering for the big fight against the fort. Already we have 300 warriors. Twice that many will be here when we ride. I am war chief. I can't leave."

"Your children are hungry. We will hunt the best we can with the older boys. We have no place to sleep, no robes, no cooking pots, nothing but fresh coals to keep in our sand tin until we start our next campfire. Where will we be safe from Captain Two Guns?"

"What of Yellow Wolf?"

"He bravely tried to defend us. He fell in the first volley of shots from the rifles of Captain Two Guns."

"I can't leave here. This alliance has taken so long. We have so much depending on a killing strike at the Pony Soldiers."

"What shall we do? Should we move to another camp? Should we make shelter of tree boughs until our warriors return?"

Running Bear screamed into the afternoon light. Other warriors looked at him.

"If I go, all the others from our band will go. If some of them go, it will hurt our unity here."

A dozen of the warriors from Running

Bear's band approached him cautiously.

"Is there bad news from Waiting Woman?" one asked.

Running Bear nodded. Soon he told them. One by one the men turned and walked to his war pony and his small supply of food and supplies.

"They are returning to the burned out camp," Running Bear said. As soon as the other warriors heard, they rushed away in groups and singly.

An hour later another rider came into the camp. He was Cheyenne and had been wounded.

As soon as his tale was told, the entire Cheyenne band picked up and rode away, north toward their own camp that had been destroyed by Captain Two Guns.

Running Bear told his woman to return to the camp site with her brother. If the alliance broke down completely, he would follow soon.

Running Bear stayed two more days at the site of the gathering of the tribes. No other bands arrived, even those who had told him personally they would be there. Alliances were always hard. All of the Brulés and Oglalas had arrived. Only the one Cheyenne and none of the Arapaho groups.

At the end of the two days, Running Bear made a count. He had only 170 warriors. Not nearly enough to do the work he had outlined.

Wearily he told the other clans that the alliance had not worked, they would attempt another meeting later in the year when the tribes were more settled down.

Running Bear's heart was heavy as he mounted his war pony and began the two day ride back to the new camp he had told Waiting Woman to set up on the Solomon. He had no idea what he would find there. They would need to rebuild their whole camp, tipis, weapons, everything. That meant a buffalo hunt for hides for tipis before the winter. More hides to be tanned into warm robes. They would need long tipi poles from a forest. Everything the Brulés lived with would need to be made.

This would be known as the summer the camp was destroyed.

As he prepared to return to his band, Running Bear found five of his warriors who were waiting for his decision before they left. They moved north together.

They decided to look for some white eyes to raid before they rode back. Then they would not show up empty handed. They angled to the east, crossed the hated steel tracks of the railroad and soon came to the Saline River.

Down river they found a small ranch and killed everyone in sight, scalped them and burned the buildings. They left with twelve horses, and moved on downstream.

From a small rise, Running Bear saw the hills blinking at him. The blinking seemed to come from many miles away. They advanced cautiously and soon spotted a half dozen Pony Soldiers on a small hill working with some kind of device they had never seen before.

Running Bear signalled that they should move up on the soldiers. When Running Bear and his men opened fire, it was with two rifles and four bows and arrows. Five of the eight men were killed in the first volley. One man struggled to the device and began sending out a signal.

"Attacked. Five men dead and . . ."

Running Bear's rifle round killed the signal man before he could continue. The other two men were promptly dispatched and their rifles and pistols and ammunition gathered up. Curious, Running Bear thought, that only one horse was found. They took it and now swung straight north and to the west where they would find their destroyed village.

* * *

At Fort Hays, Colt was informed of the partial message. He read it twice, then called for a rescue patrol. He took fifteen men and they rode faster than even he thought possible. They galloped for a half mile, then let the horses breathe with a walk, then galloped again.

The relief patrol covered the fifteen miles in slightly over two hours. It was near dark. Colt found the scene as he feared he would. Everyone shot down to a man. The mirrors on the heliograph were smashed, the device itself battered by logs the men had been using for fire wood. It would never function again.

"All of the weapons and ammunition are gone, sir," Sergeant Ivanar reported. "The one horse is missing as well."

Wearily, Colt ordered the men to dig graves. He collected the personal effects of each man and marked them plainly, then the men were laid to rest and Colt said a short service.

It was past midnight when they returned their horses to the paddock at Fort Hays.

Colonel Adamson had waited up for them.

"All dead?" he asked.

Colt nodded. "The arrows looked like

Brulé, can't be sure."

"We're sure. A survivor of a raid upstream five miles from the blinker came in. Reported he was in the field bringing in a stray when six Brulés attacked his small ranch. Killed his family and two hands. Burned everything to the ground and ran off his dozen horses. They were Brulés he knows by the way they were dressed."

"If they were raiding, they weren't getting ready to come at the fort. At least we're ready if they come."

Colonel Adamson pounded his fist on the desk. "I hope to hell something holds them up. I'd hate to go down in history as the only Commander ever to lose a fort to an attacking Indian force."

"First they have to get together. They might be having trouble talking three or four tribes into forgetting their old hatreds and work together."

"For our sake, Colonel, let's hope so," Adamson said.

The next morning, Colt sent out listening patrols. They consisted of six men each. He angled them out on compass bearings six directions from the fort. They were to ride out for two hours, then hide in the best available cover and watch and listen for any signs of a large Indian force moving toward the fort.

Colt went with one of the teams and they remained in place all day. Two hours before sunset, the troops moved out and rode back to the fort.

None of the patrols had seen or heard anything out of the ordinary. They saw no Indians at all.

That night Colonel Adamson ordered double guards be posted all around the fort. The Sergeant of the Guard was given special instructions.

When morning came, all was calm, no attack had been launched.

Colt sent out fresh men in the same six compass directions. This time he stayed at the fort. He spent some time on the roof of Barracks Two, having messages sent and received from the two outposts still in operation.

Neither had seen any Indian activity, no smokes, no sign of a large Indian gathering.

Colt sat on the roof near the heliograph and scanned the horizon with a pair of field binoculars. He wished for a twenty power telescope. As it was, he could find nothing unusual.

At last he went back to the Fort Commander's office, instructing Corporal Nelson to maintain a check every hour on the hour with the two outposts.

"Nothing! Not a damn thing out of the ordinary out there anywhere we can see. So why else would all the warriors in two camps leave their women and children almost defenseless? It had to be to go on a big raid. It must be a combined raid, since there's nothing else in this area fit to fight for with that many men. So where the hell are they?"

"You sound like you want them to attack us," Colonel Adamson said.

"Not so. I'm just afraid they will. Not exactly that. Maybe that they were going to but something happened to stop them. If we get by two more days with no large scale attack on the fort, I'll be ready to decide that for some reason they called off the whole operation."

"Your destruction of those two camps could have had something to do with it."

"Maybe. I hope so. Then who hit those two ranches upstream on the Saline River and our listening outpost?"

"Your renegades?"

"Doubt it, they were Oglalas," Colt said.

"Could have been some of the troops going back from a gathering that turned out not to be big enough. The troops wanted to strike out at something, some white eyes. They hit whatever they found.

"Let's leave it at that, Harding. You relax

a little, get some good food and a fine night's sleep and we'll take a look at the whole hostile situation in the morning."

11

The next day Colt sent out his troops on what they were now calling "picnic" patrols. They rode out two miles in six directions from Fort Hays and sat and watched.

At the end of the day they rode back in without any sight of the Indian force. When they heard the scouting report, Colt, Colonel Adamson and Major Bainbridge lifted a toast of bourbon and branch water in the Fort Commander's office.

"Our attack alert is officially over," Colonel Adamson said. "I don't know what really happened. We probably never will know, but we survived the threat."

"We have one more threat," Major Bainbridge said. "I didn't tell you during the emergency. I felt that it could wait a couple of days."

"What threat is that?" Colonel Adamson asked.

"Millicent Kane. She wants a discussion meeting with some of her people and some of ours. She says it's her right to confront the army with the way it is 'ravaging the countryside and harassing and indiscriminately slaughtering the native American Indian people.'

"I told her I would bring it up with the Fort Commander and give her a reply today."

"Out of the frying pan . . ." Colt said softly.

They all laughed.

"We'll have to give her some kind of an answer."

"Tell her that the U.S. Army is under no obligation to respond to civilian critics. Tell her we operate under the laws of the United States, and if she does not like our activities, she has recourse to her U.S. Senators and her Congressmen to change those laws. That should hold her off for a while until she forgets about it."

"I'll meet with her group," Colt said. "I had a discussion with her one time before. I think it's time these bleeding hearts understand how the American Indian really operates. Tell her I'll be glad to meet with her group tomorrow."

Colonel Adamson took a drink from his glass and shook his head. "Harding, you really like to take punishment. Wouldn't catch me anywhere near that bunch with a Gatling gun."

Major Bainbridge made a note on a pad of paper. "Get a message off to her by nine A.M.," he said. "Noon is when I take Juliana to the east bound train. She's decided that she has to go to Chicago because of Lieutenant Danalaw. I can't convince her that she had nothing to do with his death. That young lady has grown up a lot in the last two weeks."

The Major nodded and left the room.

The next morning at ten, Colt tied up his horse outside the same house where he had talked with Mrs. Kane before. Two buggies and two other horses were there as well today.

Mrs. Kane greeted him at the door, but her face was stiff and angry. She only nodded a greeting and led him into the parlor where six people were seated. He had seen most of them around town. The introductions were quickly done, and Colt knew he would not remember the names.

There were three other women, two in their forties, one younger, and two men Colt hadn't seen before. Both wore proper suits and stiff collars like they were on their way to church. One of the men wore spectacles.

Mrs. Kane took the floor. "Colonel Harding, we have just recently been informed that you and your men swept down on two helpless Indian villages, murdered a dozen people, drove the remaining women and children into the wilderness and then systematically burned and destroyed every tipi, all the stored food, every item in the whole camp. Is this true?"

"Absolutely. Mrs. Kane, do you believe in the Biblical law of an eye for an eye?"

"Yes. It's in the Bible."

"Are you also aware that among the four tribal groupings of Indians near this area, mostly to the north and west, they have accounted for 34 murders of settlers and immigrants? We have no record of the dollar value of the barns, homesteads, businesses and other buildings that the savage American Indians have burned to the ground.

"You probably knew most of the people killed, including the Freenings. You must also know that Megan Freening is still missing and assumed to be a captive of the Brulés. Can you think of anything that would be more painful and terrible for a four year old girl?"

There were some gasps of surprise from around the room. The town marshal was not present today.

One woman sniffed and looked at him. "But you do admit that you killed Indians in those villages and destroyed all of their housing and goods."

"Correct. We operate under army regulations which are stipulated by the Congress of the United States. If you don't like the way we function, it's your right and duty to tell Congress and change the laws."

"But you're *killing human beings,* murdering them," Mrs. Kane burst out almost crying.

"We are punishing those who have killed white settlers and emigrants on wagon trains."

No one said anything for a moment.

"How many of you have ever seen an Indian, not counting Daylight, the boy who was killed?"

Only two held up their hands.

"My point is, you really don't know what you're talking about. You're talking in abstractions. I can show you bullet and knife wounds on my body that are not abstractions. The bandage on my head is my souvenir of an ambush attack by a renegade band of Oglalas little more than a week ago.

"Indians are not children you need to protect. They are savages who have a whole different set of values and standards than you do. Indian warriors are bred to fight, to kill, to burn, to raid the enemy. The enemy now is the white man, or perhaps another tribe. Indian warriors kill for a living the way you women cook and sew and keep house for a living.

"Using your own moral standards as the judgment basis, every Indian male is a murdering, raping arsonist who would be hung in a moment if he were doing the same thing here in Hays as a white man."

One of the two men in the group, who Colt had not met before, lifted his hand. "But didn't we steal away all their land? I'd fight for my land, too, if I were them."

"What we do now won't change the past," Colt said. "Of course we took over the Indian lands. They didn't *own* it the way we think of ownership. They merely rode over it, hunted on it, and went somewhere else when the mood moved them.

"The whole point is the here and now. If the Indian can't learn to live by the white man's morality, then he faces one of two alternatives. He must be penned up in a reservation and be supported by your tax dollars, or the entire Indian nation will be at war with the United States until they are killed off or until they no longer are a threat to the peace of every community such

230

as Hays, Kansas."

"Isn't that a drastic measure?" one of the woman asked.

"Go see Mrs. Freening and her daughter who were both raped and then killed and scalped by Indians. Ask them if we should take drastic measures. Talk to the family wiped out on the Saline River five days ago by a band of renegade Oglala Sioux, and ask them if we should take drastic measures.

"Now, I had my say, it's your turn."

Colt listened to the people talk. Several of them asked him questions, and seemed willing to hear about the primitive society in which the Indians lived. He told them of his life in the Oglala Sioux camp. They were interested, but even then, some did not believe him.

Two hours later, he watched the last of the visitors leave Mrs. Kane's house. She touched his arm and asked him to wait a moment. When they were gone, she took a deep breath, and shook her head slowly.

"I never thought I'd be saying this, but I think what you're telling me is finally getting through. I'm starting to understand why the Indians are such a big problem. They want to live their own savage lives, but they can't do that when they mix in with the white man's culture."

She walked to the window and looked out, then came back. "You've made me understand a lot these past few days." She reached up and kissed his cheek. "Thank you." She stood there close to him, then put her arms around his neck and kissed his lips, a warm, demanding kiss.

When she stepped back she was smiling. "Colonel Colt Harding, I am a realistic woman. I saw your wedding band. I also know you probably haven't seen your wife for months." She took a deep breath. "If you'd like to . . ." Millicent began to shake her head. "No, no, I didn't think you'd be interested in seeing my bedroom. The offer stands. Those army bunks get mighty lonely." She leaned forward and kissed his lips again, gently, then walked to the front door.

"It was good to have you stop by again, Colonel Harding."

Colt saluted her, put on his hat and walked out the front door to his horse. He rode back to the fort slowly. He had informed a few, convinced perhaps one or two, but it was a tough fight and he was glad he was out of it.

For just a moment he remembered the vibrant woman's lips on his and wondered what might have been. He was happily married. He pushed her from his thoughts.

That afternoon Colt caught up with Lieutenant Garland and Sergeant Ivanar at the rifle range. The men were shooting their ten rounds, and the scores were improving.

Next came the smokeless fire test and half the men passed it and had their names marked down. The others would have to try the next day.

For the first time, the men tried riding past a bale of hay with a cardboard box tied to it and fired under their horses's neck. They used pistols first. Some of the men were catching on to the idea and the balance. It would take some time.

Back at the fort, Lieutenant Garland said he had one more man drop out of the troop. He said it was too tough.

"Strange thing is, the harder we train, the more the men seem to like it. I think they realize that the better their skills are, the better chance they have to stay alive. We also have more men's names on our waiting list. When will we cut down to our authorized strength of 50 troopers?"

"Not at least for a month when your training is over. I've made out a list of additional work for the men. You'll probably need Short Grass and his scouts to help you.

Your men need more tracking work and hand-to-hand fighting with knife and rifle as a club. Short Grass will be a big help here."

They talked well into the night about what other work the troopers needed, how it could be accomplished.

"You also need three more good Sergeants, who want to be in the troop. Talk with some of the noncoms and try to recruit them. Once they get in, they'll be pleased."

The next morning Colt sent a wire to General Sheridan in Leavenworth. Briefly it said: "Work here finished. Looking for new assignment. Detailed reports to follow in standard dispatch case."

The rest of the morning he wrote out his report of the activity in the Fort Hays area, the Indian population, the try at the alliance and what he thought happened. He finished about noon and let Colonel Adamson read it.

"Thought you should know what I'm telling Phil," Colt said.

"Sounds like you're getting ready to move on," Colonel Adamson said.

"Bound to happen sooner or later. Hoping to get to go back to Leavenworth to see my family for a while."

"Don't count on it. You know Phil Sheridan."

"True."

Three days later things still remained calm around the fort. The Lightning Troops training continued, with Short Grass taking a more active part.

Colt had time to think about little Megan Freening, the small blonde girl kidnapped by the Brulé. He was in no position to do anything about it. The band might be halfway into Nebraska by now or into Colorado. It was a concern that would never leave him. He knew first hand of the agony of a lost child, and even though the parents were dead, he still felt a powerful surge of emotion each time he thought about the small girl.

In the morning dispatch off the train, there was a large envelope for Colt from P. Sheridan. He opened it quickly.

"Orders!" he barked at Colonel Adamson. "Orders for me." He scanned the carefully written hand.

"I'm ordered to Fort Wallace out on the end of the train tracks for some reason or other. What's out there anyway?"

"Not much of anything. I don't know who's in command now, just changed."

"Fort Wallace is about 100 miles due west

along the Kansas Pacific Railroad to something called Sheridan. Then evidently about
50 miles more on horseback."

"No Leavenworth?"

"Not a chance. General Sheridan says
there's an 'immediate need' for me to pro-
ceed directly to Wallace."

"So much for the family."

"I'll leave on the morning train, and I'd
like to requisition a horse and saddle. This
train usually carries a cattle car, I'd guess."

The next morning Colt found that the
train did have a car where he could tie up his
mount. He found three other army mounts
there. They were for men who had been assigned to Fort Wallace as well.

"We'll ride out together," Colt said.
"That way I don't get lost." The men
laughed. Two were Privates and one a sea-
soned Sergeant named Haddenberg.

Colt found a seat in the coach car. There
were no first class cars on the struggling
Kansas-Pacific. He settled down with a
Chicago newspaper and began to devour every story. He should have had a newspaper
sent to him on the train from Chicago every
day. Now that chance was gone.

He stared out at the western Kansas prairie. It was cut by numerous rivers as they
worked their way west at 35 miles an hour.

It was an unbelievable rate of travel. They could move in two hours what it took a Lightning Troop a twelve hour day to accomplish. Somehow it seemed unfair.

There would be no stops between Hays and the end of the line. Colt had brought along a half loaf of French bread and a six-inch round of hard salami. It should last him the three hour ride to Sheridan and onto the end of the line.

To his surprise, Colt dropped off to sleep. The click, click, click of the rail joints and the constant and gentle swaying of the coach, acted better on him than a rocking chair.

He roused once and looked out the window. There was little change in the countryside, still the western Kansas wilderness plains, where several thousand Indians called home, and where they were rapidly being removed.

He thought for a moment of the "Indian Lovers" meeting back at Hays. The people involved simply had no factual information about Indians. They were relying on half truths and emotion to stand up for savages they didn't even understand.

They rounded a small curve and headed down a gentle incline when suddenly the car lurched as the engineer slammed on the train's brakes and the steel driving wheels locked and began to skid on the steel rails.

Colt grabbed onto the seat behind him and braced his feet against the seat ahead.

A woman in the car screamed.

"Damn, what's happening?" a man's voice shouted.

"Brakes! Hold on!" another voice came.

Just then the engine hit something. The jolt, the sudden stop and the grinding and screaming of steel on steel tore through the car as it stopped within a few feet, then twisted, slammed sideways and dropped off the tracks and tipped crazily.

The car held only about twenty people, Colt had guessed when he first came in. He didn't see the enlisted men who had taken the next car in the two coach train.

Now the car shook, then tipped more and rolled over as it left the tracks and rolled twice down a slight embankment.

Colt felt himself tossed into the air. He tried to grab something but the seat spun over his head. He slammed into the roof of the car, which was now the floor.

Colt lunged to the side, grabbed the top of a window and as the car continued to roll he caught the back of a seat and held on. He managed to cling there as the car did a second complete roll, then came to rest on its top.

Women screamed.

A baby cried.

One man swore.

Colt sat up on the ceiling of the car and looked around. Half the windows were broken out. He moved to one which was now nearly chest high. With the butt of his army issue pistol he smashed the rest of the glass out.

A woman lay nearly at his feet. She wasn't moving.

"Miss, you can get out this window," he said. She didn't respond. He bent to look at her and saw the strange angle that her head lay. Her neck was broken and he was positive she was dead.

Colt edged up and through the window, cutting his leg as he slid across some glass. Then he was outside and dropped to the ground.

Train cars lay twisted and tumbled like a child's toy. The engine was ahead, completely off the tracks, hissing steam as it lay on its side.

He helped a man out the window, then checked the door at the end of the car. He slammed it with his boot and soon had it open. Five people came stumbling out, one screaming that he had a broken arm.

Colt stepped back. The whole track was littered with cars and glass and torn up rails and ties.

He had lost his hat somewhere. Colt, in his uniform, went to the front of the train. He had to walk around the first car which jackknifed off the tracks on the other side.

In front of the engine he found the problem. A two-foot thick log had been jammed between the ties. Two of the wooden supports had been hacked apart and cut free, then a hole dug and the log pushed under the rail. A second log had been thrust through the rail on the other side to form a stiff barricade that would stop a steam engine. It had.

Colt looked up the tracks. The engineer couldn't see the problem until he was fifty feet from it as he came around the curve. No wonder he hadn't stopped in time.

The conductor was unhurt and quickly organized the trainmen. One of the civilian's horses on board the cattle car was saddled and a trainman rode away toward Hays. They were fifty miles from Hays. It would be a two day ride for him.

The cattle car had not left the tracks. It was far enough back that the bulk of the damage was already done and the force of the sudden jolt absorbed.

Colt went back and pulled his army mount out of the car. He saw the three other army men doing the same. One of the privates had a gash on his forehead, but he ignored it.

Sergeant Haddenberg rode up and saluted. "Sir, looks like we'll have a longer ride than we figured."

"Looks that way, Sergeant. My name is Colonel Harding. We'll make up a detail of four to move on to Fort Wallace. Are your two men fit to travel?"

"Fit and ready sir, but what about our gear?"

"Can you tie it on in back of your saddle?"

"Yes sir."

"Let's see if we can find it." Colt remembered his small carpet bag that he had taken with him into the passenger car. He worked his way back to the car and found the bag and his hat. He looked over one seat and saw the young woman who still lay there. He checked. Her throat had been cut by flying glass. Blood had drained everywhere. She was dead.

Colt crawled back out of the wreckage. The conductor had most of the people off to one side under some trees. He tried to organize things. Three men were sent to a creek

241

to bring drinking water. He had a former nurse helping to bind up wounds.

Two men were detailed to find the dead and bring them out of the cars as quickly as they could. The engineer was dead, as was his fireman.

The conductor shook his head. "Never saw one this bad. Whoever put them logs in there sure as hell knew what they was doing. Looks like some of the sabotage we had when we was trying to get the transcontinental across Utah back in Sixty-Nine."

Colt rode up, his gear lashed on, his hat in place.

"Conductor, I and my three men will be leaving you and riding on to the end of the line. We'll send back a rescue train. We might make better time than the one riding in the other direction. What's your name? I'll tell them you're in charge."

"I'm Amos Bushmiller. You can tell the station master that we have about twelve dead, near as I can tell. We might find one or two more. He'll know what to do."

Colt tipped his hat, pulled his big black around and rode back to the troopers.

A moment later they were on their way, riding west into the setting sun. They stayed near the tracks but in the open prairie.

Sergeant Haddenberg came up beside

Colt and scratched his head.

"Pardon me, Colonel for asking, but what we gonna do for supplies? We got no beans or bacon or any hardtack."

"We do what the Indians do, Sergeant. We live off the land. You have a .44 on your hip and a carbine in your boot. I'll expect each of us to bag at least one rabbit before the sun goes down. You ever try to eat a whole spit baked rabbit by yourself, sergeant?"

"No sir. Hope I can shoot straight."

"You don't shoot straight, Sergeant, you don't eat."

"Yeah, I been figuring that. Leastwise I'm not dead. We lost four dead in our car. Mostly from glass. Glad I didn't have a window seat."

Colt nodded and they rode toward the sun. There would be time enough later to look for game. Right now he wanted to get some miles under the hooves.

Fort Wallace. The only thing he knew about it was that they were having more and more raids and harassment by the Indians up there. They'd have to be Oglalas, Brulés, Cheyenne and maybe some Arapahoes. Same ilk he had been working against down here.

Colt knew there was going to be a fall and

winter campaign against any hostiles not on a reservation. That could mean action all over western Kansas and the eastern half of Colorado. The post at Fort Wallace would be in the center of the storm.

Colt saw a pair of rabbits ahead munching on some wild clover. He pulled his Spencer, and fired, worked the lever and fired at the second. Both spun backward into the fresh green grass and lay still.

"We'll all eat tonight," Colt told them and they rode out to pick up their supper.

Later that night Colt rested on his one blanket under the starry sky. Fort Wallace. What was in store for him there?

He thought about Doris and the kids back at Fort Leavenworth, but quickly put them out of his mind. Too much thinking about them was bad. It was better to think about his mission, and Fort Wallace.

Another campaign, another adventure!

We hope you have enjoyed this Large Print book. Other Thorndike Press or Chivers Press Large Print books are available at your library or directly from the publishers.

For more information about current and upcoming titles, please call or write, without obligation, to:

Thorndike Press
P.O. Box 159
Thorndike, Maine 04986 USA
Tel. (800) 257-5157

OR

Chivers Press Limited
Windsor Bridge Road
Bath BA2 3AX
England
Tel. (0225) 335336

All our Large Print titles are designed for easy reading, and all our books are made to last.